FALLING
FOR THE
PIED PIPER

To Win a Dark Heart

A Villainous Twist on Beauty and the Beast and The Pied Piper

ASHLEY EVERCOTT

To Sam,
Thank you for all the late nights spent geeking out over fandoms—and our mutual weakness for villains who finally got their happily ever after.

1

Selene ignored the prick in her heart, refusing to allow her one mistake to destroy her.

Illuminated by the harsh, cold light blinding her from above, sweat beaded and fell into her eyes as she squinted to make out the towering, half-shadowed High Stewards glaring from a dais. The five leaders of the Arcane Stewards sat like imposing sentinels upon tall crystal thrones, framed by stained-glass windows adorned with five-pointed stars. Blue flames wavered in the golden chandeliers, casting a glow against the marble pillars inlaid with azure crystals. The tiered benches, stacked high toward the vaulted ceiling, were filled with hundreds of stewards—leaving not a single seat open. The circular gallery seemed to close in on her, and the tiny patch of floor she stood on suddenly felt even smaller.

It was the first time a member of the Rosendale family stood before the High Stewards' judgment.

Whispers slithered around her, suffocating the air. The seven families of the strongest magical lineage were all in attendance, perched above her like sneering gargoyles. Among the crowd, she sensed her mother and father were watching too, for the unmistakable chill of her father's glare bored through the side of her face.

Selene clenched her fists to quell the tremor running through her arms. She would not give power to her fear.

Supreme High Steward Lysandriel raised her staff, and a resounding *bang* rang through the chamber when she slammed the bottom of it into the ground. Three stars at the staff's tip glowed like orange embers before fading into white. The crowd fell silent under the Supreme High Steward's command. The trial had begun.

Short, silver coily hair framed the woman's dark complexion, and her deep, indigo eyes glinted in disappointment. Selene inwardly cringed.

"Members of the Arcane Stewardship, we will now convene in judgment. May the accused step forward?" Lysandriel announced, her voice deep and commanding.

Selene obeyed. The marble chilled her bare feet, and the ragged, sweat-stained prison dress dragged over the floor. The material made her skin crawl. Nonetheless, she stood before the leaders with her head held high.

"Selene Rosendale," Lysandriel started, "you are here to answer for your crime of cursing a prince without authorization. How do you plead?"

"Guilty."

Murmurs and gasps echoed around the chamber.

High Steward Vesperian scowled. His gray hair swung when his head snapped in Lysandriel's direction. "See? She pleads guilty. She deserves a punishment fitting of her crime."

High Steward Ismara, seated beside Vesperian, frowned. "And what punishment do you feel is worthy?" Her voice, soft as a lamb, somehow traveled through the room.

Selene waited for someone to break the heavy silence that blanketed the room, but the only sound that came was the rising drum of her heart.

"Exile," Vesperian said. "Or the Nulling. Perhaps both."

Selene schooled her features into a calm mask. Stripping away her magic would be taking the very essence of her soul. She could not afford to lose everything.

Ismara hesitated. "Maybe there's another way we may deal with this. Stripping her of her magic is a severe punishment."

"And so was cursing a prince into a beast!" Vesperian countered.

Murmurs of agreement swelled through the gallery, inspiring nausea to churn in her stomach. She thought she saw the smallest twitch of satisfaction on Vesperian's lips. Like he took pleasure in the fact that he could end her whole life with but a few words.

Her jaw ticked under her gritted teeth.

"Perhaps we may agree on a compromise?" High Steward Thalandros offered.

Selene exhaled a silent, relieved breath through her nose. Two out of five High Stewards leaned toward mercy, and she only needed to convince one more for a majority vote.

"Compromise is an unacceptable mercy when she broke the balance of the magic that we uphold!" Vesperian snapped, and his sharp, amethyst eyes flashed to her.

Selene would not cower under his scowl. She had always thought Vesperian to be too harsh. He'd proven how stubborn and unyielding he could be as a professor. He always gave her lower marks on her exams when she knew she had the correct answers. They just simply weren't the answers *he* wanted.

Ismara's worried expression caught Selene's eye. The woman's pink hair was swept in an elegant updo, and light crow's feet emphasized her round, brown eyes. Although kind, Selene knew the woman was too merciful and weak. She never understood why Ismara had been chosen as a High Steward only ten years prior. However, Ismara appeared to be one of the keys to escaping the Nulling, and for that, Selene was grateful.

But of all the High Stewards, Selene respected Lysandriel the most, and now there was nothing but sorrow etched in the woman's frown. A sting ached in Selene's heart. She had wanted nothing more than to make the First Steward proud.

"Let us ask the accused for her story before we judge," Lysandriel said, and the rest of the High Stewards fell silent. "Why did you curse Prince Leander?" she asked her.

Selene steadied her trembling hands and tilted her chin higher. "Your Stewardships," she began, hoping the formalities might appease them. "Thank you for allowing me the privilege to speak. After graduating from my studies, I was most utterly grateful to have had the opportunity to be placed in the Evarandor royal court as their personal steward. When His Majesty the king and his queen left on political matters, I was tasked with staying and counseling their son while they were away.

However, after their untimely demise in their travels, the prince lashed out in grief and abused his powers. Servants were mistreated and subjected to cruel punishments, and his subjects were turned away when they needed him most. There was no time for a proper approval when the prince's rampage continued to worsen. So, I gave him one last chance."

Selene paused and took a steadying breath. "I disguised myself as a beggar woman at his door and offered him a rose in exchange for lodging. But he turned me away and called for his guards to throw me out onto the streets."

Selene's gut turned, but she forced herself to finish what she had rehearsed since the day she was imprisoned. "I acted on my good conscience to punish him."

Vesperian shook his head. "You acted without sanction!"

"I aimed to restore balance," she said coolly.

"She is remorseless," Vesperian growled, pointing in her direction.

A stinging sensation tore through her feigned confidence, but she steeled herself.

Lysandriel raised her hand, and Vesperian took a step back. The woman's eyes bored into her, and Selene swallowed the knot in her throat.

"Do you truly believe you acted in the name of justice?"

Selene unflinchingly met the Supreme High Steward's gaze, hoping it would be enough to persuade her. "Yes, I do."

Thalandros sighed. "We must concede to Vesperian. Her act was unfounded and may have consequences for the entire kingdom of Evarandor. Who may rule them while their prince is a beast?"

Selene gritted her teeth. Thalandros had always been spineless and followed whoever had the loudest argument among them. She could not allow him to falter now.

"While I understand your concern for the prince's actions," Ismara said gently, addressing Selene. "We do not condone unsanctioned curses, for we are the stewards of balance. Curses are irreversible and have the potential to cause great damage."

Lysandriel nodded. "Yes, you should not have taken this matter into your own hands. You must face the consequences."

Selene's heart sped beneath her ribs. Cursing Prince Leander was the first time she disobeyed the protocols ingrained in her. Surely, they couldn't punish her too harshly if this was her first offense?

High Steward Kallisar hummed, and his sapphire hair glinted against the light like a sparkling dagger. Selene's eyes darted to him, her mouth pinching into a tight line. It had been suspicious how he hadn't said a word up until this point. He must have been silently gloating over her predicament as she stood before them in judgment.

His position should have been hers. She didn't understand how this by-blade brat had been chosen as High Steward after the last one had passed.

For as long as she could remember, they had been rivals. They competed for the highest marks in their studies and good standing among the Arcane Stewards. No matter how hard she tried, he seemed to be one step ahead of her, even winning Crown Scholar by half a mark.

Kallisar's smooth voice broke through her thoughts.

"Perhaps banishment, or other extreme methods, don't need to be resorted to," he said, with a measured tone. "Selene is one of our most talented stewards, and wasting such talents would be a shame. However, it seems she has no comprehension of the term 'justice'. Perhaps we may teach her. What if we give her a task—to atone for her crime?"

Selene's nails dug into her palms as she glared at him. Who was *he* to teach her anything?

Lysandriel considered this with a thoughtful expression. "What do you propose?"

Kallisar leaned forward with the faintest gleam in his eyes. "There is a rogue who does not abide by our rules of magic. It has come to my attention that he must be stopped—his use of wild magic is reckless and dangerous."

Whispers spread through the chamber, but Selene attempted not to show her curiosity.

Kallisar continued, "I believe he goes by the name of, the Pied Piper."

Sharp gasps erupted from the crowd, and the High Stewards exchanged glances. Ismara frowned while Vesperian remained impassive.

Selene narrowed her eyes. The Pied Piper was nothing but a vagrant who busked the streets. Wild magic was taboo, and those who dabbled in such chaotic forces were placed on the Arcane Stewardship's watch list. However, it was technically not illegal unless the user harmed others, and the Piper's use of it extended only to charming his audiences and occasionally ridding the area of rat infestations.

What was Kallisar thinking?

He had never stuck his neck out for her before. Their rivalry had been filled with subtle jabs, but here he was, offering a lifeline instead of a sentence.

"No one has been successful in tracking down the Pied Piper. He has evaded all our stewards," Ismara said, looking to Kallisar.

"He's too dangerous," Thalandros added. "It would be a fool's quest."

Whispers of agreement rose in the air, and Selene's curiosity piqued. What did the vagrant do?

"But he must be stopped and brought to justice for his crimes," Kallisar said, his fists clenching. "Last week, he abducted one hundred and thirty children from their homes, and they have yet to be found. We must do something before it's too late."

Another wave of outraged utterances echoed around her. Selene's eyes widened. Anger slowly simmered beneath her veins, and she ground her teeth together. Had they not imprisoned her for two weeks, she would have been privileged enough to know about this atrocity.

The faint echoes of her failure reared up to taunt her, reminding her of the image she had shattered with a single act. Her hands clenched into fists.

"For once, I agree with Kallisar," Selene said, projecting her voice. All eyes landed on her. "Send me to find the criminal. Let me prove myself worthy."

Silence settled over the gallery, and the High Stewards regarded her with stoic expressions. A bundle of nerves swarmed in Selene's stomach, but she held her rigid posture.

"Do you believe such a task will pay for her crimes?" Vesperian asked Lysandriel, breaking the silence.

Lysandriel exhaled slowly. "I believe it is a fair compromise. There must be order and balance in all things, including the consequences for our actions."

Selene's breath caught as Lysandriel turned to her, her dark eyes ablaze with authority.

"For your crime of bestowing a curse without the proper sanctions, you will apprehend the Pied Piper," she decreed. "Your criminal act must be compensated by bringing true justice upon another. However, your magic will be suppressed to prevent further harm to others. Your wand will be confiscated in our care."

Selene's brows creased. They had already taken her wand when they imprisoned her, but a vortex of shimmering, yellow light burst in front of the dais. Her wand, which she had carried since the beginning of her schooling, floated above her head. Its crescent moon tip gleamed under the chamber's brilliance. It glided into Lysandriel's open hand.

"Let this be a lesson to those who believe they may serve justice on their terms."

A sharp pulse of magic surged through Selene's shoulder. Fire burned through her flesh, but she gritted her teeth to hold back her pained screams. In moments, it was over, and she glanced at her arm.

A brand.

Selene had seen it before—one that weakened a magic user's power, warping every spell into something unreliable and unpredictable. It was the five-pointed star representing the Arcane Stewardship with a jagged line down its center. The mark of disgrace.

Holding her arm, Selene glowered up at the High Stewards. "How can I capture the Pied Piper if my magic is limited?"

Vesperian smiled—cold, sharp, knowing. "You will find a way," he assured her.

"You will have three months to apprehend the Pied Piper and bring him here to answer for his crime," Lysandriel said stoically, staring back at Selene's scowl. "Fail, and we'll send more capable stewards in your stead. You will lose the remainder of your magic and what is left of your name."

2

Mother and Father did not wish her goodbye at the gate. She knew they had stayed in guest rooms within the Arcane Sanctum since they attended her trial, but their absence now left a hole in her heart wider than the brand marking her as an outcast. Instead, guards escorted her into the dead of night, in cold silence and with even colder glares. Selene kept her head held high, despite the knot burning at her throat as she trekked alone. Not even her family wanted to see her.

The word *failure* echoed in her thoughts, but she shoved it deep within the recesses of her mind. Eventually, the word became as distant as the Sanctum's gleaming white towers.

She would prove herself worthy again.

Hours later, after sleeping in a dingy inn, mud clung to the delicate chiffon of Selene's dark violet skirt and stained her matching, heeled boots. With each squelch beneath her shoes, she mourned the ruined leather. Selene had never traveled anywhere on foot, and the ache in her feet continued to remind her of that fact. Her leather pack, filled with rations, clothes, and the funds she made as a royal steward advisor, sat heavy on her back. The job had paid handsomely, but her stomach clenched at the reminder of Evarandor.

Shaking her head, she forced herself to keep walking even when her muscles screamed in agony. The pain became the distraction she needed from the darkness shadowing her wandering reflections.

Fog swirled around her steps, blanketing the green hills in soft gray. The sodden, grimy road led to a clearing where a silhouette of a village appeared out of the fog. Rolling hills dotted with wildflowers and dense woods encircled the quaint town. Soon, she could make out small, gabled structures and matching gabled windowsills. As she approached the entrance, a sign with the words *Hamelin* swung from an iron hook on a wooden post.

The High Stewards couldn't provide further details about the Pied Piper, so she wasn't about to go into this task blind. She only had three months to capture him, and if she was going to succeed, she needed to know precisely what he had done and how.

Mud soon gave way to narrow, winding cobbled streets. Faded yellow buildings with ochre, timber-framed fixtures loomed on opposite sides as she navigated toward the village square. She eyed the closed shutters and the darkness shrouding every window. At nearly eight in the morning, she suspected it was usual for commoners to be up and about to sell their wares. She'd visited bustling capitals filled with a cacophony of dizzying sights and sounds: shouting vendors, children's laughter, and hammers striking anvils in smitheries. But in Hamelin, empty wagons were parked in front of empty stalls, and an eerie silence bore down on the cobbled square.

Not a single soul was milling about.

Selene shivered. There was a strange, dark aura about this place that she couldn't quite put her finger on. Was it the Pied Piper's doing?

Then, a strange sound caught her attention. Across the square, she spotted a lone figure striding toward a building with a large ring of jangling keys attached to his person. Quickly, she approached, and the man stiffened, his thin face paling at the sight of her.

"Excuse me, sir," she said, slowing before him. Her voice wavered at his suspicious glare behind his greasy, gray locks. "I'm here to investigate the Pied Piper. Can you point me to someone I may speak to about what happened here?"

The man's sneer melted like ice under the sun's radiance, and a smile bloomed in its stead.

"Oh, you're one of the stewards, right?" he asked.

"Yes, I am."

"Then follow me to my office," the man said, opening the door for her to enter. Pastel blue walls lined with carved, wooden borders were adorned with floating bookshelves, and a polished, cherrywood desk sat at the back of the room. A cuckoo clock carved with cheery squirrels and acorns ticked the seconds down, but she noticed the time was off by two hours.

"Come inside," he said. "I'm Burke—the mayor of this town. How may I help your investigation?" He sat at his desk and motioned for the plush chair opposite him. Selene eyed the lacey doilies under an inkwell, a bell for calling servants, and a wooden bowl filled with brightly colored candied fruits.

"You may have one, if you'd like," Burke said and nudged the candy bowl in her direction.

She gave him a tight-lipped grin instead. "Perhaps later. Unfortunately, my time is limited, and I must gather as much information as possible before apprehending the criminal. When did he arrive?"

Burke let out a long breath as he sank into a chair. "Well... it happened about a week ago." He rubbed his hands together, his face drawn with exhaustion. "We had a rat problem—a terrible infestation. They got into everything—chewed through our food storage and were spreading disease. We were desperate. Then this young man arrived shortly after, offering his services. He promised he could rid of them."

"And you accepted?"

"Of course. He led them right out with that magic pipe, and we never had a problem since."

"What did he look like?"

Burke hummed in thought. "Tall, with dark reddish hair, and orange eyes. Wears an odd patchwork of clothing. He seemed nice enough, but we heard rumors about this odd fellow from a neighboring town, that this was one of his usual tricks to lead rats into towns and scam them of their money. So, we were reluctant to pay him for his services."

Selene nodded, understanding the frustration. She wouldn't have wanted to pay a fraud either.

"When he asked for payment, we refused him," Burke continued. "Told him we weren't about to be swindled by some con artist. And he stormed off, furious. Told us we'd regret it. We didn't think much of it." Burke expelled a heavy sigh. "Then, the next morning... the children were gone."

Selene's brows furrowed. "Gone? How?"

Burke's face darkened. "That cursed pipe of his. It seems that he can hypnotize more than rats. He... he must have used it on them. One hundred and thirty-one children, led away in the dead of night."

Selene's stomach turned. "And you haven't found them?"

"Not a trace."

Selene sat back, perplexed. A whole week, and not a single child had been found?

"We are desperate to get them back," Burke insisted.

Selene couldn't shake the image—over a hundred children, walking, entranced, with no will of their own. Was the Pied Piper keeping them hidden somewhere? Or were they too late in saving them?

She didn't know, but she was determined to find out.

"Where is everyone?" she asked. "I didn't see anyone in the village."

Burke sighed. "Still grieving. This town has never felt so lifeless before."

Selene couldn't imagine it—losing a child. The darkness over the town made sense in retrospect: the whole village had been affected by this tragedy.

Selene clenched her hands beneath the table, her resolve hardened. She would find the villain even if it meant going to the ends of the world to hunt him down.

She stood suddenly. "Thank you for explaining the circumstances to me. I will succeed in finding him," she promised.

Burke nodded, his expression grim. "And when you do, let me know. Send a pigeon, and we will make sure justice is served."

Their eyes met, and Selene caught the gleam in the mayor's gaze—something too eager, too sharp.

"Rest assured, the Pied Piper will face justice, but at the hands of the High Stewards," she said coolly. The irony in her statement was not lost on her, but she could not risk losing her magic or status among the Arcane Stewards forever.

"Of course, miss," Burke said, bowing his head. "However, if you feel so inclined, I believe the folks of Hamelin would like a say in how the villain should be punished. Surely, they've earned it?"

Her fingers twitched at her side as she considered him. He hadn't raised his voice, yet something beneath his words felt like a coiled snake ready to strike. Something in her gut told her to ignore his question.

After a moment of uneasy silence, he said, "But, I wish you luck on your journey!"

Selene shook the unsettling feeling aside. Perhaps the mayor had been personally affected by this loss, or the weight of all one hundred and thirty children sat like an iron yoke upon his shoulders. In any case, she empathized with the vengeance she sensed beneath his measured tone.

With one final nod, she spun on her heel to commence her hunt.

3

After twenty taverns, fourteen false leads, and a crack in one boot, Selene had failed to locate the Pied Piper.

A deep ache ran through her legs as she climbed an incline in the road. She had thought perhaps her muscles would become used to the walking she endured throughout the month, but the terrain had not been kind to her or her wardrobe. Selene stopped counting how many tears and frayed ends of her dresses she found and gave up mending them. No matter how much she bathed in the taverns, dirt nestled under her nails, and a film of cheap soap coated her skin.

What she wouldn't give for her silk sheets and perfumed oils.

Selene rubbed the back of her neck, where pain spread through her shoulders. The pack she carried seemed to weigh heavier each day, and for a moment, she wondered if someone had enchanted it to make her journey increasingly miserable.

However, the worst of her discomfort lay beneath her pride. Shame reared its ugly head at her failure. Her father's disappointed glare flashed through her like a streak of lightning. This journey was meant to redeem her, and she had nothing to show for her efforts. She'd wasted one month already. Only two months remained before her time was up, and no trail, sound of a pipe, or rat was in sight.

Somewhere, out there, she sensed the Pied Piper was laughing at her.

Gritting her teeth, she soldiered on, spite fueling her steps as she reached her destination atop the hill. She marched past the gates and pushed past a bustling crowd.

A drunken Brownie she met at the previous tavern had sworn he'd seen a strange fellow with a pipe heading toward Velmira. Although it wasn't much of a lead, something was better than nothing.

The shops became a blur as she marched down the streets. She frowned when she glanced at three people digging into trash down an alley. Murky water, grime, and slanted buildings lay beyond the opposite end of the passageway. She quickened her pace, hoping to escape this part of town.

When Selene turned the corner, she froze. Soft, lilting music drifted above the crowd like tinkling laughter catching on the wind. The notes were warm like shimmering sunbeams breaking through the stormy clouds in her mind. The purpose of her mission faded, lost in a breathless moment of wonder.

The sensation mesmerized her, and its gentle coaxing pulled her along on invisible strings. Selene followed the sound and a trail of people to a large, open square. A small, wooden, covered stage sat in the center, and she stood on her tiptoes to peer above the crowd.

The song's melody took flight, stealing the very breath from her lungs. It made her chest ache at the beauty and joy filling her soul, reaching into the hollow places she had long forgotten.

She hadn't felt anything like it in years.

Selene continued forward, squeezing her way past enchanted onlookers. Once she made into the village square, she finally saw him:

Tousled, dark red hair glinted with deep violet undertones in the sunlight. It curled around the nape of his neck, and stubborn strands fell effortlessly framing his temples. Smoldering, amber eyes twinkled with mischief as he commandeered the stage.

A rich red velvet vest sat snugly on his lean chest, and a loose white shirt billowed at his arms. Dark trousers and boots adorned his long legs as he moved across the platform. But when he paused for breath, his smirk drew her eye.

It was both maddeningly charming and roguish.

The final note lingered in the air long after he removed the pipe from his lips. The crowd roared with applause and cheers, but Selene did not. He bowed deeply, throwing his hands behind him dramatically before standing. Then his amber eyes met hers, and he winked.

The spell was broken. Every muscle stiffened. Her pulse pounded against her ears. After weeks of circling the country, she knew this was the man she had been searching for.

As Selene stepped closer, her gaze locked onto her target. She had expected a villain who lurked in the shadows and lured children with false promises and ominous music, but this man exuded light.

He raised his pipe to his lips and began another song, moving in time with every beat and playing as though the instrument were an extension of his soul. He was not just performing—he was the embodiment of his music.

And then there was that infuriating smile again. It flashed every so often, hinting at a lazy confidence and mysterious allure.

She despised it.

She despised how he disarmed the crowd, who were unaware of the influence he held over them. But most of all, she despised how she had been tempted to surrender to the music—to him. She refused to be charmed again.

Selene shoved through the crowd, ignoring the glares and the occasional person shouting "Hey!" in protest. She pushed to the front, stopping at the platform's edge, glaring at the man before her. If he had any sense, he would surrender now.

Selene squared her shoulders. "I order you to stop!" she called out.

The Pied Piper kept playing. He did not glance in her direction, ignoring her completely.

Her patience snapped.

She cupped her hands and shouted, "By the power of the Arcane Stewards, I place you under arrest!"

The music came to a sudden stop.

The crowd fell silent.

The Pied Piper finally lowered the pipe from his lips and tilted his head. An easy smile played on his face as he stared at her like she was a fascinating specimen.

"Wow, I'm impressed," he said, his velvety voice laced with a touch of amusement. "Arrested and publicly shamed? You sure know how to charm a fellow. Do you introduce yourself to all men like this, or am I just special?"

Chuckling rang through the audience. He strolled toward her and plopped on the stage's edge. Selene's hands curled into fists. Every eye was on her.

"Is she a steward?" someone whispered.

"I dunno, I don't see a wand," another said.

"You heard me. You are under arrest. Now get down from there," she snapped.

The Pied Piper shrugged, unbothered. "Now, why would I go and do something like that? If this is about the tavern in Wendgrover, I swear the pig was intoxicated before I got there." He made a show of placing a palm over his heart.

Selene clenched her jaw. "I command you to remove yourself from the platform at once."

He gave her a measured once-over, pausing over her empty hands. "Ah, let me guess. Lost your wand? Or did the big five take it from you? I understand if this is a bad day for you, but you certainly can't be taking it out on me."

A man next to her snickered loudly, earning him a glare. She stepped closer. "You are accused of abusing wild magic, kidnapping, and disrupting the magical order."

"Oh," he said, mockingly. "So, the usual?"

Another wave of laughter swept around her, inspiring a deep flush to color her cheeks. Selene's teeth ached under her clenched teeth. Just because she didn't have her wand didn't mean she was any less of a steward. She'd show them all who they were dealing with.

With a scowl, she raised her hands and summoned her magic. The brand had wedged a dam within her core, stifling the magic from flowing easily when she called it. It was like chaotic noise rushing in her veins.

Selene imagined chains to shoot out and bind him, but a stream of sparkling bubbles floated through the air.

The crowd roared in laughter.

"This is not a joke," she ground out as blood rushed to her face. This was not going how she had planned.

Bubbles danced around the giggling Pied Piper. "Not to burst your *bubble*," he said as he popped one with his finger, "but you are the laughingstock of the show thus far."

Before Selene could retort—or blink—he leapt up. One moment, he was lounging lazily on the stage's edge, and the next, he was twirling his pipe around his fingers like a thief toying with his shiny blade.

"Speaking of fun," he said. "How about we play a game?"

Selene sneered. "How about not?"

"Ah, but that's not playing fair, Violet. You can't come to my show, all pretty in lace, without playing my game."

Selene bristled at the pet name after the lavender hair she swept into a pristine twist this morning. Eyes narrowing, she stomped up the steps of the stage. She was ready to physically restrain and throttle him. He took two graceful steps back.

"Now you're getting too hasty. I haven't even explained the rules yet."

"I don't care for your stupid—"

"It's simple, alright?" He said, dancing out of reach. "Must say, you're a more violent violet, aren't you?"

"Just spit it out!" she cried.

"Alright, alright," he said, raising his hands. After a pause, his lips quirked into a wicked smile. "The rules are simple—catch me and I'm yours."

With a wink, he bolted down the platform steps.

Selene gritted her teeth. She hated running, hated sweating, and hated chasing down criminals. She raced after him, her boot heels clicking against the platform. The crowd parted for her, neither interfering nor offering help. They whispered and watched with interest as if this were all a part of his show.

Her breath came in sharp gasps, her lungs aching as she pushed forward. He veered left into an alley with his pipe to his lips. A soft melody flitted in the air, and she followed.

Only to scream when a swarm of bees suddenly appeared before her.

Selene skidded to a halt, pivoting sharply to avoid them. Where did they come from? Panting, she spotted the Piper climbing a house and leaping from one rooftop onto another. Sweat trickled down her neck as the looming, dark cloud of bees surged toward her. Their stingers pointed menacingly, fully prepared to sacrifice their little lives to disrupt her pursuit. No matter where she turned, they followed, and her eyes widened.

These weren't any ordinary bees she happened to run into. That by-blade rat had summoned them.

Selene's irritation flared into rage. Her jaw screamed in protest from her grinding teeth as she summoned any magic to obey her.

Finally, raw, unrefined energy flared into her fingertips like untempered flames.

The Piper continued leaping from rooftop to rooftop above her. The sun glinted against his cheeky smile, and her lips curled. There was no time to think—she must act now if she hoped to catch up with him.

Selene shot a binding spell behind her, imagining a ball of metal to encase the bees. The energy shuddered, twisting from her grip before blasting in an unflattering *squelch*.

A thick, gooey substance rose from the ground, forming a wall. The horde of bees slammed into the sticky surface with a *splat*, some trapped, others bouncing off, and flailing to the ground. Selene gaped at her horrendous creation. The transparent pink gelatin wobbled precariously toward her, smelling faintly of raspberries.

A peal of laughter pulled her gaze upward. The Piper stood doubled over, slapping his knee in uncontrollable amusement.

"I must say, using dessert as warfare is a new one for me," he called out to her.

Selene's nostrils flared, embarrassment searing her skin. He hadn't kept running, which meant he believed she had no chance against him. With a frustrated scream, she aimed another blast of binding magic in his direction. She didn't care what it did, as long as it wiped the smug smirk off his face.

The sparkle of purple magic flew toward him. His eyes widened, and instead of ropes to bind him, instead of anything remotely useful...

A white, puffy cloud materialized above his head and rained flowers.

The Pied Piper peered at the petals fluttering around him before barking another laugh. "Tell me, Violet—Is that a new trick they taught you in school, or was that a happy accident?"

Selene narrowed her eyes. "If you surrender now, I'll take it easy on you."

He scoffed, flicking a petal off his shoulder. "*Easy*, you say? Well, sorry to be the one to tell you, but you'll have to do much better than that."

With that as his parting, he took off again.

Selene growled, hot in pursuit. She threw spell after spell after him, hoping something would work in her favor, but every single one turned into something absurd.

One spell became an explosion of strawberries rolling off the roof. Another became pillows to cushion his landing when he jumped onto another roof. And another blasted honey, coating the tiles in a sticky mess.

That, ironically, was what finally stopped him.

The honey slicked beneath his boots, and he slipped, arms flailing before he crashed onto the angled roof. With a surprised grunt, he rolled down the tiles of the roof until landing on his back in the middle of the road.

Selene finally caught up, panting, her heart pounding. She loomed over his sprawled figure, his clothes a sticky blend of honey, strawberry, and petals.

The Piper tilted his head up, blinking at her innocently. "Bravo, Violet. That was a good run," he said hoarsely.

Fuming, she placed one boot on his chest and leaned in. "Surrender. Now."

"No, I don't think I will."

Before she could react, he whipped his pipe out and began to play. Red magic curled around her wrists and ankles, clamping them together. No matter how hard she struggled, her body locked in place, forcing her to fall backward. She braced for impact, but something soft and pillowy cushioned her landing instead of the cobbled stone.

She blinked in surprise, wondering why he would summon something to soften her landing. Two scuffed boots appeared before her, and she strained to look up at the smug man squinting down at her.

"I will find you," she growled.

"Is that a threat I hear?"

"It's a promise!"

"Oh, I look forward to it, Violet," he said, crouching to her level. He reached over, and she flinched, but instead of touching her, he fluffed the pillow beneath her. "Until we meet again." He waved, flashed a roguish smile, and disappeared down another alley.

4

Nothing brought out coin faster than flattery, and a man too drunk to remember his own name. The half-giant sat across from Reid, staring blearily at his cards as though they were written in ancient runes. The man's hands were large enough to snap Reid's neck, but he held the comically small cards between his shaky, meaty fingers.

Reid, known as "Kurtis" for the evening, sat back in the tavern chair looking over his hand of cards with his uncovered eye. The other bore a black eye-patch—one of his favorite disguises—while a large, brimmed hat kept his face in shadow. His coat was a dusty patchwork of colors, his jaw unshaven, and his hands covered in moth-eaten, fingerless gloves.

An iron lantern swung low above their heads, and smoke haloed the room from a dying hearth. The tavern was filled with music Reid was familiar with: raucous laughter, clinking of ale tankards, and whispers in shady corners. Some drunken fool slumped over the table, snoring softly while drooling over his pottage. Barmaids giggled too loudly over lame jokes to earn extra coin. It was the type of place one could disappear into for a few hours and regret it in the morning.

Reid's chair wobbled over the uneven stone floor. One leg had been replaced with a thick wood block that didn't match the others. Whiskers tickled Reid's cheek, and he tilted his head to acknowledge his rat friend. Petunia stood on her hind legs on his shoulder, her pink nose sniffing the air curiously. A small, brown, burlap cloak he'd made for her adorned her slender body, stopping mid-belly. Her hood was pushed back as she scanned for threats in and around the tavern.

Rain pelted the doorway when two cloaked men entered. Reid's eyes flicked to the door, wondering if a certain Violet would storm in. They played their cat-and-mouse game for three weeks, and somehow the stewardess would find him when he least expected it. At first, he was impressed by her tenacity, but after week two, he began to tire of running. For once, he wanted to sit down, enjoy a drink, and play a drunk man out of his money.

"Oi, nice rat you have there," the half-giant said, his words slurring.

"Thank you, she's a beauty, isn't she?"

"Aye. She has a cute little dressy thing on her."

Petunia's ears angled outward, turning a deeper shade from their usual pink.

"She thanks you for the compliment," Reid said, laying a card down.

"Ah, not as good as this one," the half-giant said, placing a crow on his deer.

Reid expelled an exaggerated sigh. "Well, this isn't looking good."

"Heh, s'that bad?" the half-giant asked with a lopsided grin.

"Yes," Reid said before showing his entire hand of cards. "For you, my large friend."

The half-giant's eyes bulged, "A King's Folly," he whispered as reverently as one could for being inebriated.

Reid reached over to the pile of coins and gathered them in his arms. "It's not your fault, Lofty. Luck loves me... or hates me, depending on the day."

The door burst open, crashing against the stone wall. The room shuddered at the impact—a tankard toppled over, and every head swiveled toward the figure looming in the doorframe. The wind roared, and a flurry of rain whipped inside the tavern. Candles flickered, silhouetting the woman's frame like a ghastly ghoul.

Petunia's whiskers twitched against Reid's jaw as the sopping wet woman strolled in. Limp, lavender hair dripped onto the floorboards, her blue eyes ringed with smudged black makeup, and a scowl painted her pretty pink lips.

"Luck definitely hates me," Reid murmured, holding back a chuckle at her bedraggled state.

Quickly, he stuffed the coins into his bag. From his peripheral vision, the stewardess marched straight to the head bartender, asking him some questions. The balding man drying a glass tilted his chin forward, and Violet followed the path toward Reid's direction.

Her eyes narrowed.

Well, spell me sideways.

Reid avoided her gaze, attempting to keep his movements casual. If he moved too suddenly, it would confirm her suspicions of his identity. He must remain calm.

"Ah, I'm sorry, my fellow giant friend," Reid said, leaning back in his chair. "I think it's time I called it quits."

"Aw," the half-giant whined. "Just when it was getting fun."

"Don't be too disappointed... here," Reid tossed a coin on the table. "Get yourself something pretty."

"Or another drink," the half-giant slurred, rubbing the coin between his fingers. The man burped and scratched his side before lumbering away to get another ale.

"Whatever your lofty heart desires! Now, let's be off, Petunia—"

"Not so fast," a feminine voice said, freezing him to his chair. Petunia squeaked and burrowed under his shirt.

The stewardess sat in front of him, taking the half-giant's spot. Reid folded his arms, forcing a comically confused expression at her glare.

"Excuse me, miss, do we know each other? Or are you here to flatter a blind codger like me?" Reid tapped his eyepatch with a smirk.

"Drop the act, Piper," she snarled. "I know it's you."

Reid couldn't fight the steel in her discernment and knew when to admit defeat. He lifted the eyepatch, "What gave it away this time? My devastatingly good looks through the disguise?"

She scoffed. "I can see through your flimsy disguises. They're not as convincing as you think."

"Neither are yours."

She raised a delicate, lavender brow at him.

"You've got something... here..." He gestured in a circular motion to one of his eyes, "and here," he said, circling the other. Then he motioned to his whole face. "Pretty much all around here."

Her glare narrowed, but she rubbed at the smudged makeup ringing her eyes like a deranged raccoon. Beneath the cosmetics, she exposed the deep, purple circles beneath her bloodshot eyes.

"Tired, Violet?" he asked, smugly.

"Tired of chasing you for weeks," she said. Exhaustion filled her voice, but he sensed a note of desperation lingering in her words.

"How about we stop our little charade and call it quits. You look dreadful."

Violet's lips pinched, her nostrils flaring. He knew the look—the one where someone wanted to reach across the table and slap him, but she composed herself. Her wet hair clung to her cheeks, and the flickering lantern light reflected off her lavender hair in a warm glow. In that moment, he would have admitted she looked ethereal—if not in a bedraggled way—if the circumstances were different.

"How about a game?" she suddenly asked.

Reid tilted his head. "I didn't think you were one for games."

"I'm not, but you are. So, let's make a deal," she said, pulling out a coin. He eyed it with interest. "Heads, I get to take you in peacefully. Tails, I will stop chasing you for two weeks."

Reid tapped his chin with his finger and hummed in consideration. A fifty-fifty chance wasn't the worst deal he'd been offered. It had been exhausting to avoid her relentless pursuit, and it would give him a decent head start.

Was there a downside to this?

His gaze flicked to the coin in her hand to the expectant expression on her face.

"Alright, deal. But I get to flip the coin," he said.

"Whatever you wish," she said with a pleasant smile.

There was something in the sparkle in her eye—the suspicious way her lips quirked as if she had him trapped in her web. But he reasoned it was just a coin toss. She had no wand, and he'd be able to sense a spell if she were to cast one. She'd need more than that smug smirk on her pretty lips and a tempting game if she were planning on anything.

He retrieved the coin and inspected it to check for any cheap tricks. "Alright, in three... two... one!"

Flicking the coin up, he followed the sight, exposing his neck. In a flash, she moved. She launched over the table, her hands shooting out before he could blink. The coin clattered on the table, spinning until it slowed to a stop. A sharp clink sounded.

Cool metal wrapped around his throat, trapping it in a vice collar. A flood of icy magic flooded his veins, rushing to his head like an avalanche of snow. Reid shivered, his hands reaching to the contraption at his neck.

His fingers brushed against etchings of runes, and every muscle in his body went taut. With wide eyes, he peered up at the stewardess who wore a triumphant smirk, and then down to the coin on the table.

Heads.

And around his throat: a collar of compliance.

Spell me sideways.

5

Selene had finally captured the Pied Piper—the man responsible for stealing away one hundred and thirty children from their homes.

A relieved, delighted laugh bubbled up her throat. She'd finally done it. For weeks, she'd attempted to play by the rules and found he evaded each of her attempts to apprehend him. If she was going to succeed, she needed to play dirty—and it worked.

Other patrons paid no heed to their shadowy corner of the tavern. Most were too drunk to notice their exchange, let alone the manic smile etched on her lips, or the shocked man across from her. The Pied Piper glanced down, his smile faltering as he touched the silver collar secured around his neck.

"Spells, you tricked me." He chuckled a dry, unconvincing laugh.

Selene lifted her chin. "You wanted to play, didn't you? I played, and you lost."

"Ah, I see. Couldn't beat me fair, so you resorted to cheating."

Selene sensed a note of bitterness and hurt in his tone, but she wouldn't take the bait from a baseless criminal. She ignored him, folded her arms, and relished her moment of victory. The High Stewards had gifted her the collar of compliance to apprehend the Piper since her chaotic magic could not aid her. The contraption was straightforward: whoever wore the collar must obey simple, physical commands from the one who had placed it on them. It was a device used as a last resort to arrest the most dangerous villains.

"Stand," she ordered.

He hesitantly rose to his feet, his limbs shaking.

"Hand over your pipe."

The Piper's hands trembled, his jaw clenching as he reached for the wooden pipe hidden under his coat. His nostrils flared when he extended the instrument to her. Selene took it and stuffed it in her pack.

"Now, sit."

The Piper sat, his eyes sharp and unreadable. "Neat trick. Will you command me to dance and stand on my head next? Would you like me to pour your tea?"

Selene put a finger to her lips to consider the tempting idea. "Perhaps later. For now... You will remain seated until I instruct you to stand up. You are forbidden from using any wild magic or harming me."

"As you command," he said extending his arms with a mocking bow of his head. "But your little collar won't give you the answers you desire."

Her jaw tightened. She hated the wry quirk of his lips—the triumph in his gaze. He was right: the collar could not compel anyone to tell the truth. She would not know what happened to the children unless he offered the information freely. Extortion was also ruled out. Under their laws, she could not torture someone under any circumstances. Justice must be served at the hands of the High Stewards under a court of law.

You learned that the hard way, didn't you?

Selene stiffened but quickly composed herself. She banished the thoughts of Evarandor and beasts away with a single shake of her head. That didn't matter. What mattered was the task at hand.

But how would she save the children? Would they be too late in rescuing them by the time she surrendered him to the High Stewards?

Suddenly, a tawny-colored rat peeked out of the Piper's shirt. Her brows pinched, attempting to make sense of its cloak. Since when did rats wear clothes?

Selene recoiled at the critter squeaking angry sounds at her. Then, it leaped onto the table, its tiny paws skittering toward Selene with alarming determination. It bared its ugly, long teeth at her.

She backed away with a squeal. "Don't let that filthy thing touch me!"

The Pied Piper snatched the animal before the rat could launch at her, cradling it against his chest.

"Sorry, Tuni," he murmured to the rat, petting its head. "We have to play nice with this one... for now."

The rat squirmed in his grasp, its hands flailing toward her, squeaking nonsense she couldn't understand.

Selene glared back. She was not fond of rats. They were disease-ridden, filthy creatures that belonged on the streets, not perched on people's shoulders like pets. But the way the Pied Piper cradled it so carefully made her pause. There was a tenderness to his touch, a protectiveness in handling the abhorrent rodent.

She should order him to release the animal into the wild—he didn't deserve a familiar when he was guilty of kidnapping—but the rat's eyes softened, rubbing its little face against the Piper. It was almost... endearing.

Almost.

"If you let me keep her," the Piper started, seemingly able to read her thoughts, "I won't fight you. Not that you'd be able to get rid of her anyway. She will follow me. She always finds me."

Selene sighed. She didn't want to deal with an angry rat stalking them while they traveled. "Fine. The rat can come—as long as you keep that thing away from me."

"This *thing* has a name, you know. Her name is Petunia."

Selene rolled her eyes. "I don't care what its name is."

The Pied Piper cupped his hand near the rat's ear. "She doesn't mean that. She has no idea how precious you are." Petunia folded her arms and nodded in agreement.

Selene huffed. He was utterly ridiculous.

How could this melodramatic nitwit have stolen an entire town's worth of children?

She shivered, suddenly aware of how drenched she was from the rain. Water dripped from her soaked hair, and her dress clung uncomfortably against her skin. Night had fallen, and it would be too dark, wet, and miserable to travel.

Finally, she squared her shoulders. "Hide the collar and follow me."

The Piper obeyed, wrapping his scarf around the collar with a flourish before his steps fell into rhythm behind her.

She approached the innkeeper, "Do you have any available rooms for tonight? I will need—" She hesitated. As much as she hated the thought, she needed to keep the villain close. She sighed in resignation. "One room."

The Piper raised a brow. "Oh, I didn't realize you fancy'd me, Violet. It explains so much." He gestured to the collar beneath his scarf.

Selene shot him a glare. "Be quiet."

The Piper's brows raised before he gave her a sly look. "Oh, quiet? That's what you'd like? Got it."

A pause, and then, "To clarify: When you mean *quiet*, do you mean like a whisper? Or does a murmur count?"

Selene rolled her eyes, huffing under her breath. She'd almost forgotten the caveat to the collar's magic—it could bind the body but not the mind. She could not force him into silence either.

The innkeeper looked between them, wary but seemingly amused by their exchange. "Yes, we have one room. Just for you lovebirds?"

"No, we're not—"

"In love?" The Piper cut in smoothly, hooking his arm around hers. "Not yet. We're in our slow burn stage. She pretends to hate me, and I pretend to believe her."

Selene yanked her arm away. "That's not true! This is purely..." She searched for the word, but came up empty.

If she admitted the Piper was her prisoner, she could rouse interest from the seedy men in the tavern. They might believe the Piper was worth a good bounty, and she'd have no way to outpower them.

"Professional," she finished lamely.

"I have eyes, miss," the innkeeper chuckled. His gaze roved over her ragged, drenched form and then to the Piper's vagrant disguise. "And there's nothing professional about this."

The Pied Piper snorted, and Selene gritted her teeth. She slammed a coin on the counter and extended her hand.

"The key. Please," she ground out.

The innkeeper informed her where to go and handed her a key, winking at the Piper. Heat flooded her cheeks as she spun on her heel. The Piper followed, whistling a cheerful tune in beat with his steps over the worn, wooden floors. Selene glanced behind her and met the rat's beady-eyed stare. The rodent glared at her, puffed up on the Piper's shoulder as though she and her master had secretly won some battle Selene was unaware of.

Selene marched on, her eyes trained on the steps ahead of her.

This is not how she had pictured her triumph: exhausted, soaked, flustered, and mocked by a rat in a cloak. As the Piper's whistle grew louder and more irreverent, Selene became painfully aware of the truth of her situation.

Capturing the Pied Piper had been the easy part, and the real challenge had just begun.

6

It was just a collar, Reid reminded himself—nothing more—just a magic trick. But the chill of it stung under his skin, reminding him of colder chains and crueler faces. A tremor ran down his spine. At least this time, captivity came with a pretty face and some mild entertainment.

Petunia stirred from beneath his coat, her nose wriggling at him. Reid sensed her agitation, and he sighed.

"I know, I know. It seems our lady justice has outwitted me," he admitted, patting Petunia's head.

The stewardess didn't even glance in his direction—of course not. Instead, she climbed the stairs with her back as rigid as the imperious code she lived by.

Reid's mouth thinned into a line. The chase had been fun when he thought she couldn't win. He'd underestimated her ability to bend her own rules and had played right into her trap. Somehow, she lulled him into a false sense of security with her high-and-mighty attitude—the kind he loved to see unravel—and he foolishly believed she wouldn't resort to tricks.

Reid knew better than to underestimate people. He'd have to play smarter moving forward.

His thoughts turned, and he wondered how to proceed. Running from town to town had kept everyone guessing, keeping them at arm's length, and he needed it to stay that way. Perhaps captivity could work in his favor.

The stewardess's soft but determined steps cut through his thoughts. She lifted her chin like a proud warrior queen who'd slain the evil beast, but her fingers betrayed her. They fidgeted, combing her damp hair or rubbing at her smudged makeup. Once, twice, and then three times, she glanced at a mirror hanging in the hallway and fussed with the paint around her eyes as they walked.

Perhaps it was vanity, but the slight tremble in her hands indicated something much more profound.

The stewardess approached their room and opened it with a graceful flick of her wrist. The door creaked open to reveal a small space smelling faintly of wet wood, tobacco, and a stale, stuffy scent of a room that hadn't been aired in a week. A small, narrow bed with a lumpy pillow lined the back wall, a hearth sat on the opposite side, and a small chest of drawers was placed beneath the window. On top of the dresser sat a basin for washing, accompanied by a sad, wilted flower in a vase. All things considered, it wasn't terrible.

The stewardess strode inside and placed her large pack on the bed.

"Sit," she commanded.

The order shot through his veins like a lightning bolt, forcing his limbs to spasm when he resisted. Pain radiated down his legs until Reid collapsed onto the floor in a heap. Petunia squeaked, racing out from his coat with her cloak flying behind her. She patted his face to ensure he wasn't injured.

The stewardess chuckled daintily, mirth dancing in her blue eyes as though she thoroughly enjoyed the show. When the sting in his legs subsided, he sat up and dusted himself off nonchalantly.

"I suppose that's one way to make a fellow fall at your feet, Violet."

"My name is *not* Violet," she said, folding her arms. "It's Selene, and you will address me as such."

"And I'm Reid, glad we're acquainted now," he grinned. "But, Selene, huh? Suits you. Sounds regal, proud... cold like the moon—but just as beautiful."

Pink dusted her cheeks, and his grin grew broad.

Selene cleared her throat, averting her gaze to the hearth. "None of that drivel is going to work in your favor."

"I'm not sure about that," he mused, "I think you secretly like it."

She fastened him a glare, but her blush deepened. Reid savored the small victory—he managed to fluster the uptight Violet.

"Here's what's going to happen," she declared, her voice clipped. *Of course, she'd change the subject,* he thought with a smirk. "You are my captive. We will travel back to the Arcane Sanctum, and you will be served the justice due to you."

Reid placed a hand on his heart, feigning a dramatic sigh. "You wound me, Violet. You cheat, slap a collar on me, and haul me away to prison." He leaned forward and lowered his voice conspiratorially. "What if you're shackling an innocent man?"

"You are not innocent," she snapped, her voice as cold as ice. "You stole away one hundred and thirty children from their homes and did who knows what to them. If you had any conscience, you'd tell me where they are and what you did with them."

Reid folded his arms, and Petunia nestled on his shoulder to mimic him. His lazy smile remained, but the corners of his lips quirked cynically.

"I love this villain angle you're going for," he said. "It makes things more interesting."

Selene's mouth pinched as she regarded him with narrowed eyes. Perhaps she was considering what level of debauchery he'd stooped to.

Finally, she turned on her heel, her wet skirts swishing with the movement. "I will have the bed. You will have the floor. You will sleep there," she pointed to the spot he sat in, "and you will not get up until I instruct you to. Is that clear?"

Reid gave her a mock salute. "Clear as a crystal ball. However, I have to ask: what happens when nature calls? I could do it here, but—"

Selene rolled her eyes. "Fine. You may get up if you need to use the restroom. You will not go near me or harm me. You will not leave the room. After you finish your business, you will promptly return to the floor."

Selene retreated behind the changing screen in the corner with a huff. When she emerged, in a dry nightgown, she blew out the single candle and collapsed onto the bed.

Reid sprawled out with exaggerated flair before Selene threw a pillow on his head, followed by a thin sheet. When he removed the items from his face, Selene had already turned on her side with her blanket cocooned around her. Reid smirked and settled on the floor with his new bedding. Petunia crawled on his chest and nestled there.

"I'm glad you're cozy at least," he whispered to her. Petunia chirped, and he gently patted her head.

Reid stared at the dark shadows creeping over the ceiling. Rain pelted the small window above Selene, and the wind howled an eerie song. The uneven wood planks of the floor dug into his shoulders, and he sighed.

Reid hadn't imagined this was how he would end his day, yet he somehow figured he would land in this position sooner or later. He couldn't delay the inevitable.

He'd dealt with worse and survived in the end. He always did.

7

Even the most pleasant voice could become grating over time, especially when the voice belonged to a villain.

Selene rubbed her temples, wishing she had her wand to place a silencing spell on her prisoner. Sunlight filtered through the leaves, creating a dappled pattern on the empty road. Squirrels darted up tree trunks while birdsong filled the air, their melodies a welcoming sound compared to the obnoxious noise behind her.

She sighed, glancing at Reid through her hand mirror. The wind had tousled her updo, and she had ordered him to stop so she could temporarily fix the issue. Reid puffed his chest out to sing another song he'd made up. Every day, and every hour, he seemed to come up with endless amounts of irritating rhymes.

He leaned against a tree trunk, his wide smile gleaming against the sunlight as he sang. If she didn't know any better, he appeared like a jolly fellow waiting patiently for her to finish, but she knew better. He was trying to get under her skin.

With gritted teeth, Selene smoothed the stray strands into the braided bun she had swept her hair into earlier that morning to keep it from falling in her eyes. She raised the mirror closer and nodded in satisfaction. The light dust of purple shadow on her eyes hadn't creased, and the paint on her lips hadn't bled outside her natural lip line. When she deemed herself ready, she packed the mirror and ordered him to follow. The crack in the heel of her boot tugged with each step against the uneven dirt road.

His baritone voice soared to the skies, smooth as honey and loud enough to startle the birds in the treetops. A flock of crows took flight when he hit a particularly high note.

"There once was a steward with bright lavender hair
Her pink lips were scowling, and her eyes were fixed
in an icy glare
A bark, a haughty command she gave
To the lowly Piper, she called a slave!"

Selene ground her teeth. Reid was proving why she was never fond of bards. At first, she assumed he'd abandon his irritating songs if she ignored him. However, after three days of travel, he proved her assumptions wrong.

"For the love of all magic, cease your annoying songs!" she barked over her shoulder.

Reid's light steps over the dirt path did not falter. A sly grin crept over his lips instead.

"For lo, she hated his beautiful song
Such spite, and her hatred strong
If only she uttered a kind word of peace
Would he ever consider to cease!"

Selene halted, her fists clenching at her sides. Slowly, she turned on her heel, her lips pursed. Reid hummed innocently, ignoring her baleful glare.

"Hop on one foot."

Reid bounced up and down, his eyes twinkling.

"Tap your nose," she ordered.

Reid obeyed, laughing like a fool. "And here I thought you didn't want a show?"

Selene growled under her breath. Would nothing faze him? Folding her arms, she watched with narrowed eyes as he hopped around like a deranged rabbit while tapping his nose. His rat peeked from his coat and held onto him with her claws, her head bobbing under her burlap hood.

"I'm a steward's jester, amusing as can be—she may glare all she likes, but she'll never take my dignity!" Reid sang, off-key this time, while maintaining perfect balance on one foot.

Selene sighed, rubbing her temples. At this rate, she'd wipe all the cosmetics there, leaving a red mark as proof of her vexation.

The rat's small face turned a shade of green, and Selene folded her arms in defeat. "Stop."

Reid followed orders, the mischief in his eyes burning brighter. "Aww... I wanted to get my exercise in for the day."

"I didn't want your pet rat retching on you. I'd rather avoid the smell."

"That's rather thoughtful of you, Violet. Never would have guessed you had compassion under all the ice."

"Ironic, coming from someone with no heart at all," she quipped.

"Just your average villain at your service," he said with a dramatic bow.

Selene's jaw clenched. This useless game of taunting was only wasting time. "Enough of this. You will cease to sing, hum, or whistle in my presence unless you wish to march backwards with your eyes crossed the entire journey."

Reid raised his hands, "Now, now, no need for threats. You could ask more nicely, and I'll comply."

"And when has being nice ever worked with criminals?"

He tilted his head, studying her with an unreadable expression. "A kind word never killed anyone, Violet. Even the ones who you believe don't deserve it."

Something pricked in her chest—perhaps it was annoyance, shame, or something else entirely. He hadn't said it with his typical sarcasm. The words came from a genuine place she didn't know existed in a single bone in his body.

And that rattled her the most.

"I stand for justice, and justice demands you pay for your crimes, not to be coddled by kindness," she said rigidly. Turning on her heel, she motioned for him to follow. "Now, come. We've wasted enough time."

Selene marched forward, refusing to look back. It didn't matter what he thought, she reasoned. He was a villain who kidnapped children, not someone she should feel a drop of sympathy for.

She braced for more of Reid's boisterous singing, but it never came.

After consulting her map, a fork in the road appeared just as it indicated on the parchment, and she picked up her pace. On the right, the forest thickened with shadows and dark, tangled brush. Meanwhile, sunlight illuminated the path to the left, where butterflies fluttered among wildflowers dotting the swaying grass. She also spotted a five-pointed star etched into a tree on the left—a sigil marking the Arcane Stewards' road.

Selene pressed onward, but the Piper's voice stopped her.

"You're not thinking of going that way, are you?"

She glanced over her shoulder. "You're questioning the stewards' path?"

"I'm questioning if they noted the pack of ogres who moved in that way recently. The folk I ran into two taverns ago cautioned me on it. And if you're so keen on getting me to prison faster, we'd go right." He pointed toward the dark, ominous-looking forest.

She turned and placed her hands on her hips. "Are you serious?"

"Hey, don't judge it so quickly. It's a little rough around the edges, but it's safe and efficient," he said. "If we're lucky, maybe we'll see some wood sprites? Doesn't that sound better than the path of doom?"

"No," she said firmly. "I also don't trust you, so we will keep going this way." She pointed to the path, where butterflies and dust motes floated against the sunbeams.

"Suit yourself."

Selene forged on, ignoring him and his self-assured shrug. It didn't make sense why he was mentioning wood sprites since they rarely appeared before humans. It was all a ploy to distract her.

"Why would you want to get to the Sanctum faster anyhow? It sounds like you're trying and *failing* to trick me."

"I just wanted to take the road where we wouldn't get eaten. And I thought the fastest way would sweeten the deal for you."

Selene rolled her eyes. She'd heard better lies by lesser villains than him.

However, the longer they traveled, the more an unsettling feeling began to sink into the pit of her stomach. Instead of warmth, the bright light of day suddenly felt exposing, like she was a vulnerable mouse in an open field. The wind stilled, the branches ceased their rattling, and the birdsong disappeared.

Selene kept her chin high, refusing to allow the Piper's lies to sow doubt in her mind. The five-pointed star was engraved on every mile marker, which proved she was on the right path according to her map. She could not falter now.

Behind her, Reid hadn't uttered a word. No jokes. No songs. A knot tightened in her stomach, but she ignored it. She would not allow his silence to unsettle her.

Something cracked behind a copse of trees.

She tensed. "Did you hear that?"

Reid glanced around, his spine rigid. "Might be an ogre."

She whipped her head toward him. "Will you stop that? There are no ogres here."

"I don't make the rules here, Violet. They are attracted to scenic roads, where travelers are most likely to be."

Selene swallowed. "But I thought they lived in... caves. Ugly, dark places."

"Shows how much you know. What did they teach you at that school?"

Honestly, she hadn't paid too much attention to her monstrous beasts studies. Of course, she'd memorized the information to get perfect marks then, but as soon as the tests were over, she tossed the knowledge to the back of her mind to never think of again. She had no plans of becoming a stewardess of arcane wildlife—her goals were much higher than managing beasts.

But she disliked the information she had retained. Ogres were massive, red creatures with sharp teeth and clubs. She had no desire to run into one.

"They taught me everything I needed to know. Now come along," she said in a clipped tone, secretly hoping her false confidence would lead them to safety. Even if she had never traveled on foot to the Arcane Sanctum and wasn't an expert ranger, she knew she was trusting the right path.

Another rumbling sound echoed behind them. She whirled around.

Nothing.

Reid turned to stare into the dense forest. "Huh. It might be following us."

Selene's stomach twisted. "What do you mean it might be following us?"

"Well, that's what they do," he said lightly. "They follow their prey."

Prey.

She did not want to think about the word being connected to her in any way. Reid was trying to scare her—

A roar bellowed. The sound pierced through her quivering heart, forcing her limbs to go numb. The ground shook as thunderous footsteps stomped toward them. The monster's large, hideous feet flattened the brush, ripping out and discarding young trees that lay in its path.

Selene's heart beat wildly against her ribcage. Her eyes widened as an enormous, red ogre burst from the trees, his spiked club raised. An animal skin loincloth draped around his torso, his stomach protruding, and a malicious gleam flashed in his black eyes. It towered over her like a looming giant.

She screamed and launched whatever chaotic magic would answer her desperate plea. The ogre's club wavered as he peered down at his body with furrowed brows. A carpet of plush moss sprouted all over his bare chest and arms, sprouting tiny white buds. The monster blinked, and Selene held her breath.

The ogre growled a low, dangerous sound when he locked eyes on her. She screeched when he raised his club once more.

Wind rushed into her ears. Strong, warm arms wrapped around her, pulling her away, but another shriek tore through her throat as a spike grazed her arm. Her silk sleeve tore, ripping from the seams. The air flattened in her chest as Reid hauled her in his arms, cradling her bridal-style, as he raced away from the ogre's reach. Selene clung to him, her hands shaking against his velvet vest.

"Give me my pipe!"

Selene's eyes flashed up at the hardened planes of his face. "But—"

His jaw tightened. "I cannot outrun him. Give me my pipe and allow me to use magic, or we will die!"

The ogre charged, his strides much longer and more powerful than Reid could run. Selene's heart sped, her mind running through a million thoughts of the consequences of each course of action. The shadow of the raised club darkened her face. Her scream lodged in her throat, but her hands dug through her pack to retrieve the pipe.

Reid feigned right. Dirt exploded from where the club struck.

"I need both my hands," he said in her ear.

Before she could protest, he swiftly lowered her to the ground. Her legs trembled when her boots hit dirt, but she didn't have time to steady herself. The ogre's roar shattered whatever composure she had summoned. She landed hard on her bottom.

"Here, use your magic!" she cried.

Reid plucked the pipe from her grasp, whipped around, and raised it to his lips.

A single, shrill note whistled in the air. The sound had an eerie quality that sent shivers down her arms until it softened into a delicate lullaby. The ogre halted, his barred teeth and fierce expression frozen in place. His black eyes grew glassy, and his nostrils flared.

The melody shifted, flitting around like a hypnotizing dance. An electric charge prickled her skin. Small flowers bloomed from the moss covering the ogre's chest, and shimmering, orange light danced around the monster like lazy fireflies. The ogre swayed, his eyes drooping as vines materialized and wrapped around his arms and legs.

Selene gaped as the monster let out a long, confused groan before collapsing forward. Dust billowed as the ogre fell face-first onto the dirt path, the ground trembling from the impact. The beast let out a loud snore.

He was fast asleep.

In the back of her mind, she was vaguely aware of the blood dripping down her arm. Her pulse continued to race as she peered up at Reid. He lowered the pipe and exhaled a breath of relief. A thin sheen of sweat glistened from his brow, and a slight tremor ran through his hands when he met her gaze.

"Don't worry, Violet," he said, his voice hoarse. "He won't be getting up any time soon. However, we shouldn't try our luck. Wild magic can be temperamental like that, y'know?"

Selene stared at him owlishly, unable to form a response. Then her gaze traveled back to the snoring ogre, the bright flowers perched on his back, and the vines binding him. From the reports she heard, she knew the Pied Piper used wild magic, but she'd never seen it wielded in such a way before. Wild magic wasn't supposed to work like that. It was a raw, chaotic force that couldn't be tamed unless the user's goal was destruction. It never listened—never obeyed. It only lashed out. Yet,

Selene felt its power electrify the air and gently soothe the towering ogre to sleep.

Was this what had happened to the children?

Panic crept in despite her years of training. Structured magic remained the only reliable magic that restored balance and could be controlled by magic-imbued wands. An ordinary pipe shouldn't possess enough power to defeat a formidable monster.

Selene looked back at the instrument in Reid's hands, and then at his pale face.

"You saved me," she said, but the words felt wrong in her mouth. "How did you do it?"

"I mean, I had to rush in and scoop you up fast before—"

"No," she interrupted him. "The wild magic. How did you do it? No steward can achieve what you did."

"But I'm not a steward. I'm just your ordinary bard who happened to be born with a connection to magic like stewards. Not everyone can afford fancy lessons like you, Violet. I was just desperate and stupid enough to rely on wild magic when I needed it. I'm not anything special."

It was true that some people could be born outside the seven noble families with a connection to magic. Among those, only a few were able to afford schooling at the Arcane Sanctum, yet...

"Wild magic is not possible to tame."

His lips lifted into a knowing smile. "That's the trick—you don't tame it. It's not something you can boss around and control. You have to *guide* it."

None of what he said made sense. It defied everything she learned about magic.

Reid extended his hand, and she glanced at it with parted lips. She hesitated. She didn't want to accept his help. She didn't want his charm or the sincerity softening his gaze.

But *he* saved her.

Slowly, she accepted his offered hand. His warm, calloused palm enclosed hers, a comforting anchor against the chaos flooding her thoughts.

When she stood, she pitched forward, but the strength of his hand held her up. She clung to his shirt, her vision dizzy. The pipe in his grip pressed against her arm, suddenly alerting her to the danger she could be in.

"Whoa there, Violet. Don't rush it. You're injured, and shock hits you harder than you think."

Her grasp tightened. "Give it back."

Reid hesitated but let out a deep sigh. "What if another ogre appears?"

She lifted her chin. "Then I'll give it back to you when that time comes. Until then, you will surrender your pipe to me. You will no longer use your magic, either."

He handed his instrument over, his mouth twitching into a frown. Her fingers clung around the smooth, wooden pipe, carefully sliding it into her pack away from sight.

Reid released her, and the warmth of his hands where they had rested around her waist lingered even after he stepped back. Selene stumbled to a tree and leaned on it for support. She took a steady breath before assessing her wound. The metal had sliced her upper arm in a clean cut, but fortunately, it wasn't too deep.

"We'll have to get you patched up soon," he said, softer than she anticipated.

Selene jolted as his finger grazed above her injury. His featherlight touch sent a shiver through her. Her heart stuttered, and her breath snagged in her throat.

His calloused thumb slid over the torn edge of her sleeve, pulling the material back to reveal the mark beneath. The five-star sigil with an ugly black, jagged line down the middle gleamed faintly against the sun.

Ice dropped to her stomach.

Selene jerked away, tugging at her sleeve to cover the mark. "I'm fine. Let's go."

He tilted his head, regarding her in a strange, quiet way. Her skin prickled under the weight of his stare.

Selene turned on her heel without waiting for a response. She didn't want to know what he might have seen—what he was thinking. Instead, she focused on the road ahead.

"Hey, Violet?" he called behind her.

She didn't turn back, but her heart sped like a jackrabbit. "What?"

"Do you think you'll trust the bard to know when to avoid the scenic route next time? I can't risk dying right now. I've got too many things to take care of before that happens."

Her lips pursed, but she didn't respond. What did he mean by that? And why did the 'things' he mentioned sound more like 'someone' he needed to take care of? Perhaps he meant he needed to make sure no one found the children. Too many thoughts and emotions vied for her attention, and she didn't wish to entertain any of them. Especially the question that was chipping at her resolve: Why had he saved her?

Shaking her head, she pressed onward, attempting but failing to keep doubt from whispering in her mind.

8

Everyone had their share of secrets—the stewardess was no exception.

Reid silently watched Selene fussing over the pile of sticks she called a 'campfire', her shoulders tense and her focus sharp on the flint she attempted to strike into a flame. He hadn't said a word after he glimpsed the mark under her sleeve three days ago—he hadn't needed to... yet.

It explained some of her prickliness, snappy orders, and the constant battle for control. The broken sigil meant only one thing: disgraced.

It turned out she wasn't the perfect stewardess she fancy'd herself to be, but that made her all the more interesting.

Reid tilted his head, studying how her brows furrowed deeper and deeper into her pretty forehead as she failed to light a flame. It had been at least twenty minutes, but she had refused to give up or ask for help. A lesser person would have given up and whined to have him do it.

So, he'd give her one thing: The woman had grit. And perhaps a bit of pride stacked on a mountain's worth of sheer willpower. He couldn't help but respect that.

The sun began setting behind the mountains, beyond the thick of trees encircling their camp. Reid sensed the energy humming through the soil, the trees, and every living creature within the forest. An ancient power pulsed within the wild magic around them, as if it were alive.

The woods held a damp, earthy scent, and Reid surmised that it had rained in the area recently. Selene wouldn't be able to get a flame with the soggy twigs she'd gathered into a tiny pyramid.

"Y'know," he started, placing his hands behind his head as he leaned against a tree, "the flint might spontaneously combust if you keep glaring at it like that."

She didn't spare him a glance, her sight set solely on the flint and steel in her hands. "I don't want your help."

"Oh, no, I'm not offering help, just giving some moral support from a safe distance."

A spark flew but quickly faded into the breeze. Selene cursed under her breath.

"I didn't know they taught you those kinds of words at your fancy school," he said. "What will the big five say?"

Selene whipped around, her mouth quivering. "For once, can you leave me alone? I'm doing the best I can!"

Reid blinked, but she had already turned away from him. He frowned, disliking the hunch of her shoulders and the piercing silence that followed. He rose and crossed the space between them. Selene didn't look at him, her hands working furiously in a scraping motion.

"Violet... I shouldn't have—"

She muttered something and dropped the flint and steel. Purple magic flew from her fingers, but, instead of fire, a green substance exploded onto the hem of her skirts.

A sharp hiss sounded, and Selene shrieked. The liquid sizzled through the material, charring the threads and releasing an acrid, bitter smell. She scrambled away, but the substance crawled through her skirt in jagged lines.

Reid lunged for the hem, holding Selene's legs steady as he tore through the silk. The fabric yielded with a pop of threads, and the acid crackled against the breeze. Reid threw the toxic material across the dirt clearing.

It landed in a heap, spitting out a plume of smoke. The acid ate through the fabric until it disintegrated into the wind. A silence washed over the clearing, save for their ragged breathing.

Her legs trembled beneath him, and her warmth seeped into his fingers. Suddenly aware of himself, he retracted his hands, disliking the tingling current running through his veins. Selene's gaze swept over the frayed remains of her silk skirt, where half her petticoat peeked through the gaping space below her knees.

"You alright, Violet?" He asked, looking her over, checking for burns.

Selene blinked at him. "What—why did you—?"

"Save you again?" he supplied. "Or did you mean ripping your very expensive dress? Unfortunately, both were unavoidable."

She half-huffed, half-chuckled as if in disbelief. Her fingers brushed against her shin, and she winced.

"May I?" he asked, gesturing to the petticoat.

"Don't. I'm all right."

Reid leveled her a stern look. "You clearly aren't. Let me at least take a look so we can see the damage."

Selene hesitated, biting her lip before saying, "Fine..."

Carefully, he lifted the petticoat to her thigh, revealing a patch of reddened, blistered skin. He inhaled a hiss through his teeth.

"You're not going to like this next part," he murmured. Before she could answer, he swept her into his arms.

"What are you doing?" she sputtered. "Put me—"

"Before you give the order," he cut in, meeting her eyes. "Please trust me on this one thing, all right? We must get you to the stream, or your burn will worsen." He stared at her, pouring his sincerity into his gaze to reassure her he wouldn't do anything nefarious.

Her lips parted before she averted her eyes. "Very well."

Reid rushed toward the stream and carefully set her down on the soft, mossy embankment.

"I'll need to take this off," he said, gesturing to her boot. "May I have your permission?"

This time, she did not fight him. She nodded, and he carefully took off her boot and peeled off her stocking, being gentle to avoid jostling her and aggravating the burn.

"Now, let your leg soak in the water for a while. It might sting at first, but trust me, it will feel better soon."

She obeyed, dipping her foot in until the water reached the burn on her shin. "Ah!" she cried out.

"I know," he said, "but give it a moment, Violet."

Finally, she relaxed, letting her shoulders fall. Reid sat beside her, watching her pained expression soften into bliss.

After a few minutes, Selene shifted while eyeing him warily. "What?" she asked.

"I'm just looking at you," he said innocently. "And thinking."

"That doesn't sound like a good thing."

Petunia skittered up to him, standing on her hind legs. She must have finished her exploration of their surroundings and bobbed her head twice within the shadows of her tiny hood. No ogres nearby. Patting her head, Reid extended his arm and allowed the rat to sit on his shoulder. Petunia squeaked in his ear, her whiskers tickling his cheek.

"Yes, I agree," he nodded solemnly.

"Agree about what?" Selene inquired.

"You're not used to this, are you? Being helpless?"

Selene's eyes rounded. Reid fought back a smirk—his assumptions were rarely wrong. But more than being right, he wanted to hear the real Violet beneath her mask and hoped he might see a glimpse of her tonight.

Selene ground her teeth. The word *helpless* sank its teeth into her gut, but she straightened. The nerve of this man—

"I'm not helpless," she shot back, but winced, hating how she sounded more petulant than intended.

He glanced at Petunia, humming like he'd heard this lie before. Even the rat looked unconvinced.

Selene huffed, crossing her arms and turning her head in the opposite direction.

"You couldn't start a fire," he pointed out. "Or realize that you can't start one on damp wood."

"Well," she stammered, "It's not like we all can be vagabonds like you."

"Oh, and I doubt you'll ever be."

Selene pursed her lips, scooting away from him. She should order him to leave, she certainly wanted to, but she wasn't a fool. It wouldn't be wise to be left alone in the middle of the night on the edge of a stream, especially while injured and vulnerable.

But a small part of her enjoyed his presence beside her—the comfort of safety it supplied.

Selene squeezed her eyes shut, hoping to stamp out the thought. It didn't matter if he saved her or tended her wounds. None of it would make him less of a villain.

"You're used to things being easy, aren't you?" he murmured.

Selene's mouth parted, her brows furrowing. The question was an observation—or an understanding, but she didn't know why he'd come to this conclusion. He didn't know anything about her.

"What's that supposed to mean?"

He shrugged, tilting his head to look at the wisteria hanging from the trees. The purple flowers swayed in the night breeze, and a thoughtful expression stole across his face.

"Just that it seems you're used to things being handed to you with spells and scrolls. All polished and full of rules. You didn't need to worry about anything except studying and memorization. You didn't have to learn the hard way."

She bristled. "For your information, I worked very hard to be a stewardess. I trained relentlessly. And just because I studied doesn't make it any easier."

His ginger eyes met hers. "Perhaps, but it certainly didn't prepare you for the uncivilized life."

"How would you know anything about me? You don't know a thing."

"I've seen enough."

Selene opened her mouth to retort, but rolled her eyes instead. She crossed her legs and hissed as a searing pain shot up her leg. She'd almost forgotten her burn. Treating wounds was also another thing she wasn't trained on without her wand, and even then, she hadn't mastered healing, but she didn't want to give him more proof of her helplessness. Even if he could probably guess for himself that she had no knowledge of bandaging burns.

She frowned, gazing into the cool, glassy water. Perhaps she had been well cared for her entire life, as the Piper insinuated. She always had a home, a place to sleep, and a position that kept her comfortable; her father could be strict, but she never worried about her basic needs.

Now, she was stripped of her magic, her status, and good standing in her family until she redeemed herself. She had nothing. Not to mention, she couldn't even start a blasted fire.

Clenching her jaw, she hated that there was some truth to Reid's accusations.

He seemed to sense her thoughts. "You get used to it," he said.

"I don't want to get used to this," she said, tearing her gaze from the water swirling around her leg. "This is not how my life is supposed to go."

Reid shifted beside her, his tone no longer teasing. "Tell me then—where was your life heading before your fall from grace?"

His question struck harder than she expected. Her throat pinched as she reached for the mark hidden under her bandages. It had been foolish to believe he hadn't seen it and recognized it for what it was. Shame seared her from the inside out.

Her lips formed a tight line, forcing herself not to indulge in his questions. She didn't need to give him any ammunition against her. Yet, something in the sincerity of his gaze unraveled her resolve like loose threads.

"My goal was to become a High Steward," she murmured. "The youngest in history."

"Ah. Sounds about right."

She fixed him with a glare. "What does that mean?"

"You're one of those climbers," he said matter-of-factly. "Always reaching for the next rung in the ladder. The kind where nothing will ever be enough, even when you reach the top."

The words stung. Selene frowned, hating how he affected her more than he should. She should have disagreed with him or ordered him away to remind him who was in charge, but the fight left her body. Instead, she stared at the moonlight rippling across the water's surface.

The conversation needed to change. Immediately.

The question she kept buried for the past few days finally surfaced. "Why didn't you run?" she whispered.

He inclined his head. "Pardon?"

"When the ogre came, you could have let me die..."

Then he would have been freed.

The influence of the collar would have ceased the moment her life ended. Silence wedged between them, filled only by the sound of the trickling stream and the croaking frogs.

"And yet... here I am," he said, his voice low. "I'm not the monster you think I am. I would never allow anyone to die under my watch."

Words escaped her as she stared at him. How could she trust what he said? What if this were an elaborate ploy to lull her into a false sense of security? But...

She still couldn't help but wonder why he wouldn't have used the opportunity to flee.

A gust of wind blew some strands of hair into her face, stirring the sweet and musky scent of the wisteria. Reid reached for her, his fingers pushing the hair back around her ear.

"You have something..." he started, but his voice waned when his fingers brushed against the underside of her jaw.

Her breath hitched. She should have pulled away or commanded him to stop, but she could only stare at his retreating hand. He raised a wisteria bloom before her.

Her traitorous heart fluttered at the simple, but gentle gesture. She shouldn't be feeling any of this—not the flip in her stomach, or the roar of her pulse.

But the sensations remained, frightening her more than the ogre had.

"Your burn has soaked long enough," Reid said, breaking the tentative silence. "Let me bandage it for you."

Selene didn't trust her voice. She nodded, and he stood to retrieve a white strip of cloth from his bag. When he returned, he dipped the bandage in the cool water and gestured for her to lift her leg. Hesitantly, she raised it, and he settled it on his knee before winding the wet cloth around her shin.

The air shifted. Her throat grew dry as she watched the pinch of his brow, the sharp lines of his jaw, and the focus in his eyes as he worked.

"You didn't have to do this, either," she said, her voice hoarse with confusion. No one had before.

His eyes flashed to hers. "I know."

For once, Selene allowed herself to wonder if there was more to this man than she had thought.

9

R eid awoke to a strange sound.

His eyes shot open, muscles tensing as he assessed his surroundings. Mist curled around the base of trees, snaking over stray detritus. Smoke clung in the air from the fire he started last night, and the cold embers kicked up in the breeze. Dewdrops glistened on spiderwebs while catching the soft, gray light.

Across from him, Selene slept with her blanket wrapped around her like a cocoon. Her hair spilled around her like the first light of dawn on the horizon. The lavender strands reflected silver against the dappled morning light. A trace of something floral lingered on her despite their days of travel. Still, the stewardess had been meticulous about her appearance and hygiene, stopping at streams to bathe, apply her cosmetics, and spraying a spritz of perfume on her wrists and neck. It amused him that she cared about such things after nearly being clobbered by an ogre, but he supposed it made sense for her character. The composed, collected stewardess who cared so much about her outward appearance, as if it kept her from unraveling.

Dark lashes curled over her soft, ivory skin. A flush of pink tinted her cheeks—perhaps from the morning chill permeating the air—and his gaze traveled to the pert shape of her lips. A small sigh escaped her mouth, and Reid imagined her dreams were as peaceful as her angelic face.

Frowning, he tore his eyes away from her, hating how long his gaze had lingered. Although, he couldn't deny that she was beautiful. Sharp, but devastatingly lovely.

And stubborn as a dragon.

It was part of why he bound her injury the night before. The burn needed tending, yes, but he knew she would never ask for his help otherwise. Pride like hers didn't buckle easily. He sensed she would have straightened her shoulders, gritted her teeth, and pretended the wound didn't bother her like she'd done with the slash on her shoulder—which she had bandaged quite poorly. But he rationalized that he wished to manipulate her to take the collar off his neck willingly.

If he used his dazzling humor, some light teasing to get her flustered, and then butter her up with sweet words, he could eventually convince her he wasn't as bad as she thought him to be. He couldn't use his pipe to bind her to run away, because he knew the collar would eventually force him back to her. The magic wouldn't allow him to be more than a few meters away from her. He couldn't hypnotize her either. Only she could choose to take it off his neck.

However, his heart whispered a different truth. He didn't need to be this considerate and tend her wounds, but perhaps, deep down, he didn't like to see her suffer.

The sound of heavy boots crunching over the forest floor sounded from afar. He froze, and Petunia's ears reared back as she sniffed the air.

"I sense it too," he whispered. An inexplicable sense of dread curled in his gut. He wasn't sure what was coming, but suspected it wasn't good. Crawling over to Selene, he clamped a hand over her mouth.

Her eyes shot open, her voice muffled behind his palm, but he raised a finger to his lips as he strained to hear the faint voices.

"We're heading in the right direction," a deep, masculine voice said. "I see his tracks going this way."

Selene stiffened beside him.

"Looks like he's not alone," said another, his voice raspy. "Probably the girl they spoke about."

"We'll dispose of her and take the Piper," a third said.

"Pity," the second said. "Perhaps she could've fetched a pretty price."

"Orders are orders," the first, deep voice said sharply.

Metal clinked, and the sound of a crossbow being cocked snapped into the silence. A flock of birds took flight, and Reid's pulse soared up his throat.

Bounty hunters.

"We need to go," he said, lifting Selene to her feet. He kicked dirt over the fire and shoved their belongings into their packs.

"Do you know them?" she hissed.

"No, and you won't want to meet them either."

"Are they after you for what you did?" she asked as she stuffed her feet into her shoes.

Reid bit back a grimace.

"We don't have time to discuss that. We have to move. Now."

Selene's mouth opened and shut within the same breath when the sound of booted steps approached even closer.

"No time for questions," he said, grabbing her hand. Petunia scrambled up his pant leg and burrowed under his vest.

Reid dashed forward with Selene in tow. She stumbled behind as they hopped over a log. He ducked under a low-hanging branch before something whined in the air and *thunked* into the fallen tree trunk. Reid eyed it for half a second with a swallow.

An arrow.

Its head was buried deep into the bark, and its quiver vibrated from the impact.

"Piper!" a man bellowed.

Reid spared a glance over his shoulder. A large, muscled man with a jagged scar carved into the left side of his lips scowled. He sported cropped, brunette hair, a dark, padded gambeson over his chest, and a gleaming sword. Reid didn't know his name or recognize him—he didn't need to. This fellow knew *him*.

"Run!" he hissed to Selene, tightening his grip on her hand.

"Kill the girl," the blonde with a crooked front tooth said. The man with shoulder-length black hair nodded, reloaded his crossbow, and fired.

Reid took a sharp left, barely dodging the arrow by a hair's breadth. Selene kept up with his strides, her eyes darting to their pursuers. She stretched a hand behind her, crackling, purple magic shooting from her fingertips. Instead of slowing the third arrow, wings sprouted from the shaft, a beak sharpened the head, and feathers grew into a mishappen form. It shrieked an unnatural sound.

The arrow-bird zigzagged in a chaotic pattern before hurtling into a tree. The bark exploded, and the pieces ricocheted in a deafening blast. The bounty hunters cursed behind them.

"Remind me never to be the target of your crazy magic again," Reid called over his shoulder.

"I didn't mean for that to happen!" she cried.

"Well, it worked!"

Another arrow whizzed past his cheek. The bounty hunters were either getting closer or their aim was improving. His eyes darted to a panting Selene. "Order me to use my magic!"

"What? What about your pipe?" she asked.

Reid yanked her to the right, leading them into dense bramble. Thorns caught on their clothes, but he refused to let them slow him down.

"We don't have time to stop unless you want to be skewered. Do you think the pipe is the source?" He laughed. "Wild magic is all around us, Violet. The pipe makes it a little easier to guide. So, order me to use it. Now!"

"Fine, you can use your magic!"

Tromping footsteps boomed behind them. Metal whined in the air, whirring like an eerie cartwheel.

The hair on the back of his neck stood. His instincts screamed to life. Reid shoved Selene out of the way before an axe sank into the ground where she once stood. She cried out as she fell.

Every nerve blazed as his eyes flashed to the grinning bounty hunter.

"Throwing steel at a lady isn't very polite," he hissed. His teeth ground together as he quickly hauled Selene to her feet. His fingers clasped around her arm, grounding her to him. He didn't wait for her next breath or a protest.

Reid jerked Selene into a denser copse of trees. Fire burned his lungs, his legs screaming, but magic surged into him like lightning. Anger guided the chaos, willing for the dense brush to open and close behind them as they fled. Roots shriveled, the bushes bending and branches drooping sideways to avoid slowing them down. Every fiber of his being screamed to protect—to escape the danger pursuing them.

A wall of stony caverns lined their new path, and a plan was formulated within a single breath. Reid called to the unbridled wild, coaxing the wind to stir.

The air swirled and shimmered until an illusion of him and Selene materialized. The shadowy versions of themselves raced forward as he tugged Selene toward a crevice in the rocks. Grabbing her by her waist, he hoisted her in, and she followed with a squeak.

Darkness suffocated them in shadows. Stone pressed into his back, and his chest compressed against hers, their breaths heaving in sync. His hand came up to her mouth as their assailants rushed past them to follow the illusion made of reflective light and wind.

"Don't let them get away!" the blonde one cried.

"We have to get back what's ours!"

Reid stiffened. His blood ran cold, and his taut muscles couldn't relax until he heard their footsteps disappear entirely. A wave of exhaustion washed over his body, making his knees buckle. He'd used more wild magic than he should have, but after a few minutes, his legs ceased shivering. When the voices finally faded into the distance. Reid released a slow breath of relief.

Then, he realized his hand was still covering Selene's mouth. His fingers tingled as he slowly pulled away, letting his hand drop to his side.

Selene inhaled sharply, their gazes locking in the dim space. The crevice was too tight, too warm, too... much.

He was keenly aware that her fingers were still curled into his shirt, and the faint scent of lavender clung to her hair. Her eyes were wide, and the same charged awareness flickered in them.

Tension crackled, but she didn't push him away.

Not that she had much room to.

Her lips parted, as if she wanted to speak—but then she hesitated. For a traitorous moment, his gaze flickered to her mouth. It was a foolish thought. Not the time. Not the place. And most definitely not the woman he should be thinking about.

Instead, he smirked, breaking the silence. "Are you cold, or are you excited to be around me? You seem to be shivering with delight."

Selene's scowl was instant. "I am not."

Except her pulse betrayed her. Reid still had a grip on her wrist, and the erratic thump of her heartbeat gave her away.

His smirk deepened. "Liar."

Her cheeks flushed. She tried shoving him, but there was nowhere to move.

Reid chuckled. "We barely fit in here. I'm surprised we even got in. Not sure how we're getting out, though."

Selene huffed. "Maybe by *you* moving."

She pushed him again. He grunted, shifting slightly to create the tiniest bit of space—not much being produced.

From his shoulder, Petunia chittered in amusement. Reid sighed. "I know, I know. Not my best plan."

Selene's glare darkened. "Just move."

She tried wiggling out of the crevice, but the rock walls pressed tighter against them. She winced, the jagged stone most likely scraping against her.

Reid frowned. "You all right?"

"Oh, this is just *fantastic*," she snapped. "This is all your fault!"

"My fault?"

"Yes!" She prodded at his chest again. "You got us in here, now get us out."

"All right, let's try this. On three, you push forward, and I'll lean back."

She exhaled sharply. "Fine."

"One," he started.

"Two," she continued.

"Three!"

Instead, he nudged her as she leaned forward. Selene yelped as she tumbled, landing face-first on the forest floor. Reid, still wedged in the crevice, burst into laughter.

Selene spun around, eyes blazing. "There's nothing funny about this! You *pushed me!*"

He raised his hands in mock surrender. "I was helping."

She brushed off her skirts furiously. "Well, don't do it again!" After a pause, she looked around cautiously. "I didn't know there would be more people after you. Why would they want to harm *me*?"

Reid shrugged, feigning nonchalance. "I don't know. But I'd rather not find out."

She studied him. "They said they want to 'get back what's theirs.' Did they mean the children?"

His muscles tensed, but Selene didn't look away. For the first time, he realized she was catching on.

Reid forced a lazy smirk, "Probably."

A flicker of concern passed across her face. She folded her arms. "Are they in danger?"

Reid exhaled, his jaw clenching slightly. "They're safe."

"Where?"

"That's between me and Petunia."

Selene's lips pressed into a thin line. "Fine. But once we get to the Arcane Stewards, we will get the answers out of you."

"Looking forward to it, Violet."

Selene turned away with a huff, muttering something about insufferable men with their thick skulls. Reid leaned back against the stone, and Petunia peeked her head from his coat with her hands folded nervously in front of her.

He should have been with the children three days ago, but the subtle hum of the collar forced him away from them.

Until then, he needed to figure out a way to escape.

10

Selene had never been more aware of her rumbling stomach or how ill-prepared she was to track her rations. Another day of travel had been wasted because of their run-in with the bounty hunters. She was forced to take the longer path, extending their travels by another week.

She was expected within a fortnight, leaving them only two days to spare if they kept their pace. They still needed to go through three more towns, cut through another forest, and then ascend half a mountain where the Arcane Sanctum sat carved into the rock.

Selene couldn't afford any more detours, but she couldn't afford to starve, either.

The silhouette of a town—Brambelune, according to the map—was a welcome sight, but unease settled in her stomach. There was no way to tell whether the bounty hunters would track them here or if they would be recognized among the crowd.

Selene shuddered at the memory of the axe that had nearly cleaved her in two. If she closed her eyes, she could taste the metal as it sliced in the air. She didn't know who had sent the bounty hunters after Reid, and she certainly didn't know who would want her dead in the process.

Something wasn't right, and Reid knew more than he was letting on.

Selene's fingers clenched into fists. It infuriated her that she couldn't order the truth out of him.

They stopped to eat the last of their rations before entering town. Reid toyed with a cracker she'd given him for lunch before offering it to Petunia, who was perched on his shoulder. The rat bobbed her head in thanks before taking the morsel from him. Her whiskers twitched as she sat on her haunches and held the cracker between her small front paws. Selene couldn't help but smile—the rodent looked adorable as she nibbled at it with small, precise bites.

"What will you eat, then?" Selene asked. "That was the last of what we had before going into town."

"What, are you concerned?"

"No," she said quickly. "I don't want you fainting from hunger, is all."

"I won't faint. I've been hungrier," Reid said, reaching over to pet Petunia on the head.

Selene stared at the wry quirk of his lips and the softening of his deep, amber eyes. Her throat grew dry at a sudden memory. She recalled how near she had been to Reid in the narrow passage, positioned between the stone wall and his firmly built frame. His eyes had landed on her lips, and their heaving breaths tangled between the fragile space. She wondered what his mouth would feel like. An inexplicable desire welled inside her to close the distance to satiate her curiosity.

It was a horrible, shameless, intrusive thought...

He was like a stubborn curse—no matter what she did, she couldn't root him from her mind. She couldn't ignore how he'd saved her life from the ogre and the bounty hunters when he had every reason to leave her for dead. If she were killed, Reid could walk away as a free man from his collar. He didn't owe her anything. Yet, he had tended to her wounds and bandaged her burns with gentle hands.

She couldn't tell if it was an elaborate ploy to manipulate her or if there was more to the man than she had once believed. He even gave up his rations to his pet rat rather than eat them himself. Was that an act as well?

The tenderness in his gaze said otherwise. He reached over to his rat when she'd finished her meal, and she grasped his finger, sniffing and chittering happily.

If Selene didn't know any better, she would have never guessed he'd stolen over one hundred children from their homes.

"She really likes you," Selene murmured.

Reid shot her a glance, his smile lifting higher. "What, are you jealous?"

Heat rushed to her face, "N-no! I'm simply surprised anything could like you."

" Touché," he said with an air of nonchalance. "I don't know what I would have done without her."

"How did you find her?"

"More like she found me," he said wistfully. "When I was a kid wandering the streets, I ran into the wrong crowd and found myself on top of a pile of trash by the end of the scuffle." A dry laugh escaped his lips. "I'd lain in that dark alley for who knows how long, perhaps waiting for the rats to take me away."

A rawness edged his voice—she sensed a wound deep within his past. It pierced through Selene's defenses.

"But then she came and sat on my chest," Reid gestured to Petunia. "She looked at me with her kind, round eyes, and I knew I couldn't give up hope. Somehow, for some reason... she chose me. And since I had no one to call my own in the world, I accepted her in return. She's been with me ever since."

Petunia yawned and curled up in the folds of his coat. Warmth bloomed in Selene's chest as she regarded the tawny rat and her tiny pink nose. She had to admit that the little, burlap cloak looked adorable on Petunia.

A part of her recoiled at the sympathy chipping at her walls, but she couldn't help but yield to the genuine display of kinship between the Piper and his rat friend.

"She's no ordinary rat, is she? They don't live that long."

"Two years at most," he said, "but I heard they could go to four if you're lucky. I was fortunate in a different way. One day, Petunia got sick, and I used whatever wild magic would aid me. It enchanted her and bonded her to me as my familiar. She's been aging slowly ever since."

Selene blinked slowly. "The wild magic extended her lifespan?"

Reid shrugged. "I can't explain why, Violet. Perhaps the Divine took pity on me. Whatever it was, I'm not going to complain. I tried leaving her behind once, thinking my travels were too dangerous. She ended up following me across four towns, hitched a ride in a pig cart, and boarded a boat to find me. The captain said she gave him a good bite when he tried throwing her overboard. I've given up trying to play the selfless hero and allowed her to accompany me everywhere."

Selene smiled softly, her gaze returning to the sleeping rat. "She's quite loyal to you."

"Not sure why," he admitted, scratching at his arm. "Don't know why she'd want to follow a half-witted fool around the country."

"It must have been nice, though," she murmured.

His gaze flickered to her with a curious glint. "Which part? The part where I accidentally enchanted her, or the part where I ended up with the most adorable rodent stalker?" he teased.

"Having a friend," she said.

Selene hadn't expected the words to slip past the barriers she had meticulously built all her life. It may have been the exhaustion she could never sleep away, or the kindness softening his eyes that lowered her guard, but the words were suddenly free.

The wind stirred the grass, whistling through the branches above. Reid's smile faltered.

Selene glanced at the half-eaten cracker in her hand. "I was too busy for friends. There were too many expectations to live up to."

She didn't elaborate on what she meant: how her father had sculpted every second of every day. He was the master of her scheduled life and demanded nothing but excellence. Everything was to be perfected: her mind, magic, and appearance to serve the legacy of her prestigious Rosendale family name. Her family had served the Arcane Stewardship for centuries, and she was expected to follow the same path. There was no time for fun or laughter. No time for friends.

Sunlight peeked through the clouds, stinging her watering eyes. She sniffed, banishing the emotions away, but some stubbornly lingered. "Excellence comes with a price, and I paid for it. Sometimes, even when people surround me, I feel the loneliest."

Selene swallowed and glanced at Reid. She had expected pity but was surprised to be met with gentle eyes, as if he empathized with the shadows of her pain even if it wasn't his own. The air shifted. Selene couldn't understand why, but the silence didn't create an awkward distance.

It frightened her.

Selene stood to her feet, brushed off the crumbs from her dress, and placed the cracker in her pocket. Clearing her throat, her cheeks burned at the slip of her vulnerability, especially to a villain like him.

"Come, let's go. Pull up your hood so you won't be recognized."

He did so without argument. "I have some disguises if you want to use them, too."

Selene rolled her eyes. "As if any of those disguises fooled me."

Reid's grin widened. "I think we might need them this time." He gestured to her lavender hair.

He had a point. Although there were bound to be people with different shades of purple hair in town, the bounty hunters would immediately recognize her. She eyed his bag warily.

"What do you have in there?" she asked.

"Glad you asked!"

He rifled through the ratty-looking bag, which was a medley of cobbled-together materials. At last, he took out something soft and silky and presented it to her.

"Tada!"

Selene grimaced and delicately took it from him. It was a short, yellow wig, the color of bright daffodils, with a shaggy, unflattering cut.

She looked at the wig, at Reid, and back at the wig. "Is this all you have?"

"I have a green one too!" he said proudly, before revealing a clover-green wig that would skim her shoulders.

Selene eyed it distrustfully, but she imagined it was better than nothing. "Fine," she sighed. "I'll take the green one."

Reid took the yellow wig and stashed it away. He retrieved a pointy hat and slapped it on his head. He then placed a thick mustache above his lip.

"See! Foolproof," he said with a grin.

Selene rolled her eyes but had to admit that he didn't look like his usual self once his deep, burgundy hair was hidden under the hat.

"When did you last use this?" she asked, eying the green wig.

Reid shrugged. "I don't know. But I think it's clean enough."

Selene frowned, not wanting to know what this thing had been through. Still, she put it on without further complaint.

She retrieved her hand mirror to inspect her new hair. The color clashed with her skin tone, and her eyes appeared dull. She sighed. "This is adequate."

Reid grinned. "I have experience with disguises."

"Is that how you swindled people? Wearing masks?" she asked.

Reid chuckled, but his voice lost its teasing edge. "Not too far from the truth. It was the only way to survive, sometimes."

A heaviness sank to the pit of her stomach. Her heart prickled at the thought of him as a boy, alone in the world, wearing different masks to scrape together whatever money he could. It reminded her of how she had to put on a mask before her father to please him—to earn her meal as well.

She studied Reid's face, but his eyes looked far away.

"All right," she said briskly, "We've wasted enough time."

"One more thing."

Reid reached into the bag, took out a delicate chiffon shawl, and moved in front of her. Before she could protest, he lifted the fabric and tied it neatly under her chin.

His finger brushed the underside of her jaw, and goosebumps rippled over her skin. Selene stared up at him, her lips parting. Reid's eyes flickered over her face with something unreadable in his gaze.

"I suppose we all wear a mask," he murmured. "Yours made you unyielding. Mine made me a villain."

Selene averted her gaze, unable to swallow the unshakable truth in his words. From her peripheral vision, his fingers reached out, and she held her breath as he tucked a strand of violet hair beneath her wig.

"There. You're all ready, Miss Pfeiffer," he said with a small smile. "And still beautiful."

A flush radiated through her chest and up her neck. She didn't know where he made up these fake names, but she hadn't expected the soft quality of his voice to make her believe he meant what he said. The wig insulted her image, yet he still found her beautiful.

She cleared her throat, stepping back. "Let's go."

"As my lady commands," he whispered.

Selene turned on her heel, hating how her heart sped like an elated hummingbird. These sensations were a trick of the imagination—nothing more, and nothing less. Raising her chin, she marched on with one goal:

Getting the spell-blasted Piper out of her mind.

11

Reid whistled a merry tune as they entered the town of Brambelune. People bustled through the market, vendors shouted their wares, and children played games near a fountain. Streamers strung from one timber-lined building to another, creating a web of bright, colorful flags dancing in the late-summer air.

Selene strode stiffly toward a stall, her jaw set, and her back as rigid as a wooden plank. The shoulder-length green strands of the wig swung with each purposeful step. They approached a booth lined with sparkling Winesap apples piled in neat rows, but he scanned the fruit with a meticulous eye. When Selene reached for one, Reid gently tugged on the back of her sleeve.

"Not that one," he whispered in her ear.

She turned, irritated. "Why?"

Guiding her away from the stand, he said, "See how they put the nice ones on top? Look at the apples beneath them—rotten, moldy. The top is for display."

To her credit, she checked discreetly at the bottom rows of apples before huffing in displeasure. "Very well. Where do you suppose we should go?"

Reid impulsively placed a hand at the small of her back, his fingers twitching subtly over the silk.

She did not pull away, and his heart gave an annoying lurch.

"Somewhere where they won't swindle us," he said, scanning the lines of stalls stretching down the street. "That one's better. And the merchant won't cheat us."

As he led her toward the orange stand, Selene scoffed. "How would you know that by just looking at him?"

Reid's mouth twitched. "I just know."

"That's not an answer."

She peered up at him with a flicker of curiosity that caught him off guard. Reid never imagined the stewardess would show any interest in him.

"When you're on the streets, you have to learn fast. You get a sense for who will curse at you and chase you off, and those who will slip you a bruised fruit when no one is looking."

Reid studied the sun-weathered man a few feet away. The vendor had a gentle smile standing behind a shaded stall. "See, this man?" he asked. "He's not shouting over everyone, his smile is genuine, and he's giving a sample of one of his oranges to that little boy."

Selene looked in the vendor's direction as the man peeled an orange for a scruffy eight-year-old child.

"People who fake kindness always want something out of you. I can tell he doesn't," Reid said. The vendor patted the boy's dirty hair before the child scurried off with his new bounty. A quarter of an orange would have been a treasure when Reid was his age.

Selene's mouth pursed in thought. "You're awfully insightful."

"Like I said," Reid shrugged nonchalantly. "It was part of surviving. I had to make a living off reading people."

Selene went quiet, and he quirked a brow in surprise. The stewardess usually had a snide quip to everything he said, but perhaps he finally said something that didn't annoy her.

"Welcome, friends," the vendor said as they approached. "How may I be of service today?"

Reid bent to inspect the ripe oranges and nodded in approval at their quality. "We'd like about five of these, if we may—"

"Seven," Selene cut in.

Reid turned to her with furrowed brows. "Is seven a lucky number?"

Instead of answering, she nodded toward an alleyway to their right, where two pairs of eyes peeked around the wall. A head of matted, blonde hair and short, brunette curls disappeared when he spotted them.

Selene averted her eyes when he glanced at her, but he understood her silent message.

"Seven oranges, please," he told the vendor with a small smile.

After Selene paid, she headed for the alley. Reid followed, curious to see what plans she had up her sleeve. The alleyway stretched between two slanted buildings, its stone and timbered walls cracked and dilapidated. Sunlight filtered between the sloping roofs but couldn't chase all the shadows away. A torn curtain fluttered above a cracked window, and a pile of broken crates. The faint stench of garbage clung to the air—a familiar, almost nostalgic scent that brought him back to his childhood.

A pair of eyes peeked around a barrel before vanishing. Reid's mouth tightened in tandem with his chest. After his grandmother passed when he was seven, he had nowhere to go and found himself as lost and afraid as the children shivering in the alley.

Selene took another step before placing two oranges on one of the crates. "It's a shame these beautiful oranges must go to waste. I hope someone can help me finish these off," she said, looking around the alley nonchalantly.

Reid blinked rapidly, taken by surprise at her gesture. Patting her dress, she returned to his side with her eyes focused and her chin lifted like a stoic knight. She motioned him forward, and Reid peeked behind his shoulder, smiling as a dirty pair of hands swiped the fruit from the crate.

The corners of his mouth curved into a smile. "So," he began, falling into step beside her. "Has some of the ice finally melted from the walls of your heart?"

Selene rolled her eyes. "Don't be absurd. We couldn't carry that many oranges, anyhow."

"I see," he hummed. "Let me know when you'll want to be charitable to me next time."

He winked, and she pierced him with a fierce glare that would wound a dragon. His grin deepened. Despite her fierce expression, an attractive shade of pink dusted the bridge of her nose.

With a huff, she marched forward to continue their shopping. Reid kept pace with her strides, his heart pounding when their hands brushed. He didn't entwine his fingers with hers. Instead, he savored the softness of her fleeting touch.

For some reason, she did not pull away.

12

S elene did not have to look to know Reid was smirking behind her. She could sense the teasing glint in his eye, the unmistakable *knowing* in his gaze that bore through her walls, like he knew a secret about her she wasn't privy to.

The oranges were a mere act of charity. Stewards were instructed to promote goodwill, and she fulfilled that duty. It had nothing to do with how she saw the ghosts of his past in the eyes of those starving children, or her sense of obligation to his acts of kindness. It had nothing to do with her heart softening toward a villain she was handing over. No, it had nothing to do with the Piper whatsoever.

Yet, the ache in her chest said otherwise.

Green hair swayed in her eyes, and she swiped it away in frustration. She straightened, throwing her shoulders back as they finished collecting their rations. Several food stalls lined the bustling street, some selling spices from faraway kingdoms, while others sold fried dough and fresh fruits as treats. Wooden figurines, jewelry, clothing, and other handmade crafts lined another street they passed.

From the corner of her eye, Selene saw a woman sitting at a small wooden table, a purple crystal ball glinting beneath a striped canopy. Cloudy blue shimmers danced within the ball, emanating a strange magic. The woman's long, wavy, dark hair cascaded over her shoulders, and golden bangles and intricate jewelry adorned her hands. She was young and beautiful, with an air of grace and mystery.

Based on her studies, Selene knew fortune tellers were swindlers, as no one could truly predict the future—but perhaps they were simply clever and highly observant individuals.

Still, she lingered a little too long, wondering where she sensed the threads of magic pulsing through the air.

Reid nudged her elbow with his. "Come on, let's try it out."

Selene's eyes widened. "Are you serious? I am a stewardess. I am *not* going to pay an impostor to read my fortune."

"Oh, come on, Violet. Are you afraid of a little fortune-telling?"

She could have ordered him to keep walking, but something whispered to her to stay. A small curiosity itched in her mind.

Before she could decide, the woman lifted a hand, beckoning them forward with a knowing smile.

"Come closer, my dears," the fortune teller purred. "What may I do for you?"

Reid tugged Selene toward the woman, grinned, and sat at one of the open chairs. A surprised breath of air escaped her lips when he pulled her into the other awaiting chair.

"Oh, we're just two sweethearts who must know how our passionate love endures through the future!" He declared dramatically.

Selene elbowed him hard in the ribs.

He coughed. "Ow."

The fortune teller chuckled as she reached forward, beckoning both of their hands. "Love is the purest endeavor. I shall commune with the magic our Divine has gifted us to find the answers you seek."

Selene restrained herself from eye-rolling. Every textbook debunked this kind of wild magic. The fortune teller's eyes closed as she hummed an eerie melody. As she swayed, a tingling sensation spread through Selene's arms. The air hummed with an electric tension—a wild and raw energy similar to when Reid commanded wild magic. Suddenly, the woman's eyes snapped open.

"I see an... unconventional love between you two," the fortune teller said, her brows furrowing as if surprised by the answer.

Selene let out an unamused scoff. "I suppose that's one way of describing it."

"Secrets run deep," the fortune teller continued, eyeing Reid. Selene watched as the knob bobbed with his swallow. Before Selene could wonder what kind of secrets Reid kept, the woman's dark eyes bored into hers. Goosebumps pebbled over Selene's arms.

"And you resist what is right before you, my dear. There are brutal truths you have yet to accept. If you deny them, you will never be free of the chains that bind you. I sense... a beast in your past. And until you accept these truths, you will never be free from the shadows of your transgression."

Her stomach twisted as the words pierced a sensitive place she had hidden behind her walls.

Does she know?

Panic crawled under Selene's skin. This couldn't be happening.

Selene forced a calm expression, but she swallowed the knot forming in her throat. If she didn't react, the woman wouldn't be able to confirm any of the nonsense she claimed.

Reid, of course, was utterly delighted.

"Chains?" he repeated with mock wonder. His hand touched his scarf where the collar lay on his neck. "Sweetheart, I think she's talking about that fancy piece of jewelry you gave me—"

Selene stomped on his foot under the table, and he hid his wince with a smile.

The fortune teller continued, her voice low and hypnotic. "If you open your heart... you will find love—"

The fortune teller paused, her eyes closing as if the universe was whispering to her.

"—and marry... a roguish bard."

Reid gasped loudly. "Did you hear that, Violet? It's a divine affirmation. What's your ring size?"

Selene gritted her teeth, ignoring him. She turned her attention to the fortune teller. "Perhaps the magic is wrong. There is absolutely no possibility I'd ever be interested in a bard."

The fortune teller nodded knowingly. "Ah, denial."

Reid clasped a hand to his chest, shaking his head in mock sadness. "You wound me, Violet."

The woman continued, "The magic cannot lie. It says the fires of passion will burn strong despite your differences."

Reid smirked and leaned over to whisper. "I think she's onto something."

"He will win you over with his kind heart."

Selene rolled her eyes. "Now I know you're wrong."

"I think you should listen," he said in a false, sagely voice. "The magic seems very wise."

Selene stood abruptly, nearly causing the crystal ball to roll off the table.

"Thank you for your—" she forced a tight smile, "—wise advice." She placed a few coins onto the table and turned sharply on her heel. "We'll be on our way."

Reid chased after her, laughing. "But I wanted to know how many kids we'll have! I bet they'll have magenta hair."

Selene stormed forward, her fists clenched at her sides.

"What is it, sweetheart?" Reid teased. "Are you denying our fated love? I mean, I already have to do everything you command. Might as well put it in writing."

"Shut up, Reid."

As they wove through the marketplace, the fortune teller's voice rang behind them.

"Fate cannot be denied!"

Selene did not look back—she couldn't—not when the fortune teller had cut through a wound that hadn't quite healed. Her thoughts raced, her heart slamming against her ribcage at the words echoing around her shame.

"I sense a beast in your past."

How would she know? The fortune teller didn't know her name or that she was a stewardess. Perhaps rumors of her crime had trickled into this town, but how would the woman know Selene was the perpetrator? Everyone from Evarandor, whom she had cursed, could not speak about what happened between her and Prince Leander. They were bound in silence—to keep the truth from ever letting out.

And Selene had planned to keep it that way.

A thunderclap cracked across the sky. A fat raindrop landed on her shoulder, then another.

Reid let out a loud laugh. "Looks like the magic is upset with you!"

Selene gritted her teeth. This was going to be a long night.

13

A flash of lightning streaked across the sky. Petunia nestled under Reid's coat, her soft, warm body vibrating against his chest, and he patted her in comfort. Tree branches thrashed against the howling wind, the leaves shivering violently like his companion, who marched on as if unfazed. Lightning streaked above the snow-capped mountains in the distance. Selene stiffened beside him, jumping at the sounds of thunder echoing through the valley. The drizzle of rain grew steadier over the golden fields of grass until it came down in a fury. Selene shivered, trying to pull up her hood, but it was useless. Their clothes were growing more drenched by the second.

Reid glanced over his shoulder. "We need to get out of this rain. We should turn back to Brambelune."

"We need to keep going. With those bounty hunters and restocking supplies, we've been delayed long enough."

"We can't travel like this," he gestured to the sky. "Not when you're shaking like a leaf, Violet. You'll catch pneumonia, and *then* you'll be late turning me in. And that's the last thing you want, isn't that right?"

Reid knew he shouldn't encourage the stewardess to hand him over to the Arcane Stewards, but he wasn't a fool about to march through a thunderstorm. Catching an illness could mean the end for both of them, and he couldn't afford to die just yet.

Rain dripped in rivulets down her cheeks before she gave a reluctant nod. Slowly, he extended his hand, and she slipped hers into his grasp. Her cold fingers trembled as he led her toward a cluster of trees. Droplets of water splashed on his neck as he scanned his surroundings and the paths diverging from the main road. In the distance, farmland stretched over rolling hills, and he tugged her in that direction.

The mud squished under their boots as they ran, and that's when he spotted it—a large barn hidden behind a thicket of trees. A homely cottage with a thatched roof, slanted chimney, and a wooden fence sat a few yards away.

"Follow me," he whispered. Selene's hand twitched, but she obeyed.

Reid located a back door and ushered her inside.

She frowned. "Someone's going to find us in here."

"Then we'll be quiet and stay hidden," he said. "We'll wait out the storm, and then we can move on."

They slipped inside, and the scent of damp hay filled his nose. Sheep bleated from a pen, cows chewed on their cud, glancing at him before resuming their meal, and an enormous pig peeked its head over its stall. Tiptoeing, Reid led Selene up a ladder to a dusty but clean loft.

"We'll hide up here," he said, once they were settled over a bed of soft hay. Only then was he acutely aware that Selene had tugged her hand out of his grasp. "Petunia will let us know if anyone's coming, and we can run for it if we have to."

Petunia squeaked and scurried out of his coat at the mention of her name. Her claws scuttled across the wood before she disappeared down the ladder. Selene nodded and removed her soaked cloak, revealing an indigo dress that clung to every curve. The silky material shimmered deeper like a blanket of twilight, and royal purple embroidery swept across her bodice in embellished waves. Water dripped from the sharp, raised edges of her pauldron, decorating her shoulders.

The moisture fled Reid's mouth, and his heart stuttered a ridiculous rhythm.

Selene huffed, taking each pin out of her wig and placing them in her lap. Once the wig was off, the cap followed. At last, she shook her hair free from its plaits, and the scent of a blue lavender breeze struck his senses.

An impulse nearly drove him to reach out and warm her hands between his own, to feel the storm beneath her walls. Selene shifted, and he refrained, knowing it was a bad idea, but he couldn't stop his hands from twitching at his sides.

"I can make it warm in here," he offered.

She pinned him with a baleful stare.

"I meant with magic, Violet."

Her lips pursed, then nodded. "Fine. Use your magic. But only for this purpose. After, you will not use a single spell until I permit you again."

On the opposite side, dusty horse blankets hung from the railing. Reid retrieved them and summoned the familiar tingling magic surging through his core. Wild magic rushed like a chaotic cloudburst before he molded it into a calm mist of rain. The trick was to guide and plead with it like a friend in need of assistance. The magic yielded, and heat bloomed through the blanket in his hands.

Reid sat beside her. "This should do the trick. It could smell better, but it'll keep you warm for hours."

She eyed him warily before wrapping the offered saddle blanket around her shivering form. He placed the other on his lap and listened to the soothing rainfall beat against the roof.

A clap of thunder boomed. The barn shook from the sheer force of power howling through the air. The sheep bleated, and Selene stiffened beside him, eyes wide, and pulled her knees up to her chest. When another crack of thunder roared above, Selene clapped her hands over her ears.

Reid's natural response to tease vanished. The way she curled up on herself, shivering and rocking, made him pause.

An ache wrung in his chest. He had never expected to see the crack in her armor split so thoroughly as it did in this vulnerable moment. Selene was untouchable, with a sharp scowl at the ready, but this new side of her stirred something raw and protective deep within him. His hands twitched, clenching and unclenching with indecision. This would be the perfect opportunity to sway her and soften her view of him—but the rational part of him screamed he shouldn't give in to the impulses, to stay clear of the feelings driving him to chase away her fears.

Thunder exploded, and when a whimper escaped her lips, it was all he needed to silence the rational thoughts.

Reid drew closer and carefully wrapped an arm around her shoulders. She startled, her head snapping up, but before she could pull away or order him to take his hands off her, another crash of thunder echoed through the sky.

Selene threw her arms around him, burying her face in his chest.

A breath snagged in his throat. Reid couldn't move. He didn't dare to breathe. His heart shuddered against his chest as her warmth coursed through his chilled skin. Her body trembled, her arms tightening around his waist, and her nails dug into his shoulder blades. Little did she know that her actions would be his undoing.

Reid slowly embraced her in return. He closed his eyes, resting his chin against her head.

Spells, how did this happen?

He realized this was no longer a ploy to sway her opinion of him for his freedom. It was something deeper—something more. He knew he shouldn't care for the stewardess. Not when she held him captive, and not when she still saw him as a criminal. By definition, it was utter madness to feel anything for the woman handing him over to the High Stewards. If this kept up, he'd be locked away for insanity on top of the kidnapping.

Yet, while her arms were wrapped around him, Reid didn't mind giving in to madness. Something clicked into place in her embrace, and he didn't want to let go.

Not now. And perhaps... not ever.

The storm continued to rage, and she gripped his shirt tighter, her body tense against his. Reid hummed a lullaby his grandmother used to sing to him before her passing. His fingers moved gently through her damp hair, his touch grazing the back of her neck. Time stilled, and Reid didn't know if minutes or hours had passed, but her shallow breathing slowed.

Light filled his chest. Somehow, he managed to do something right for once.

After the thunder finally subsided into a low rumble, Selene pulled back slightly, but she remained close enough for him to feel her warmth.

"Are you alright?" he asked gently.

"I... don't think you would understand."

He gave her a small, patient smile. "Try me."

Her eyes darted away. "There's always been something... unsettling about storms. I've been afraid of them since I was a little girl. The chaos of it... the vibration echoing in your chest, and the anticipation of the next strike, but not knowing when it'll happen next... It's just too much."

He nodded, giving her space to continue.

"I grew up in a world that was rigid," she admitted. "There was always a plan. Always perfection. I couldn't fail. Thunder is unpredictable but inevitable. Like how I couldn't fail but seemed to do so anyway."

She trailed off, swallowing hard, and he could tell there was more she wasn't revealing.

"That makes sense," he said softly. "Storms are chaotic, but you feel the strike in your bones. Perhaps you are afraid of what you cannot control... That's probably why it unsettles you so much."

Her head snapped up, eyes blinking rapidly like she wasn't sure how he could see through her that easily. "How would you..." She paused as if thinking better of it.

He chuckled. "I just pick up on things, Violet. You may put on a good front, but you're not immune to the cracks in your pretty armor."

"I have perfect control over my emotions."

He gave her a knowing look. "No, you don't. You bury them. That's not the same as controlling them. Real control is letting yourself feel without letting it consume you. It's like wild magic—you can't force it to behave. You can only guide it."

Her lips parted before shutting, all within the same breath. The iciness thawed in her eyes before she released a sigh. "How do you even do that? It seems impossible."

His fingers brushed through the silky, damp strands of her hair. "It takes practice. You learn to feel it, guide it, and let it go. It's... a kind of healing. And it's something I'm not perfect at either."

Selene scoffed lightly. "You seem perfectly adept at allowing chaos into your life."

He gave a soft laugh. "Only because I had to. People hurt me. They betrayed me. I learned to survive by leaning into the chaos, letting it move through me instead of fighting it. It was the only way to get by."

Tightness coiled in his stomach. Memories of cruel faces, cold chains, and ravaging hunger stole through his thoughts. His lips pressed into a line, willing the images away.

She glanced up at him, curiosity flickering in her eyes. "What happened to you?"

Reid let out a slow breath. "My grandmother had taken care of me all my life. She was the one who taught me everything about music. She loved petunias, the flowers that is. It's why I chose the name for my little rat stalker. But she passed on when I was seven, and I was forced onto the streets. I had to steal and lie to make it day by day. Music and magic... they didn't come easy. But once I figured it out, it became the only thing that made sense."

"That sounds terrifying."

"It was. But that's the thing about life," he said, locking eyes with her. "You can't control what happens around you. You can't control other people, storms, or... any of it. The only thing you can control is how you deal with it. How you choose to keep going."

She was quiet for a long time, her fingers absently tracing the edge of his shirt. Finally, she nodded, her voice softer than usual. "Maybe... maybe you're right."

Reid gave her a crooked smile. "Funny, I'm pretty wrong most of the time."

She let out a half-hearted huff at his joke, but she didn't pull away. A pleasant current sang in his veins when she nestled onto his chest again. Neither spoke, but he found peace in the sound of the drumming rain and the warmth of her arms around him.

14

A strong, steady beat thrummed against Selene's ear. The unwavering rhythm sang like the slow lap of waves against the shore, waking her from her hazy dreams. Something about the measured thrum grounded her in reassurance and comfort, to allow her walls to come crumbling down.

The scent of rain and a hint of black cherries wrapped in aged cedar, lingered in her awareness. Something warm anchored around her waist like a protective band, seeping comfort into her chilled skin. It felt like home.

Her lashes fluttered against her cheek, and a beam of light assaulted her vision. She winced at the sting settling deep behind her eyes, but froze when the wall she leaned against moved up... and down. A puff of air disturbed the top of her head, followed by a soft snore.

Selene jolted awake, her pulse spiking at the sudden cognizance rushing to her senses. The soothing drum against her ear was not just a melody her mind had conjured up—it was a beating heart. The weight around her waist belonged to an arm attached to the last person she should be this close to.

Reid.

She had fallen asleep in his arms, propped up against the wall. Selene's gaze flashed upward where sunlight filtered through the window, highlighting Reid's peaceful face. The dark burgundy strands of hair fell against his high cheekbones, glinting like deep, purple wine. She could count every pore and trace the lines down his lean neck—her pulse thrummed beneath her skin, attuned to his every shift, breath, and touch.

Selene didn't know how she let him get so close—how he slipped past her defenses and held her in his arms. Memories of the night before flooded her mind, filling in the blanks of her confusion. The thunder she'd always feared led her into the arms of a stranger, but deep down, a part of her whispered she didn't mind—that maybe he wasn't a villain after all.

The thought awoke the roaring perfectionist within to rear her ugly head. She'd lose her little reputation if anyone found out she had *snuggled* with a criminal. Father would be furious.

He kidnapped one hundred and thirty children and did who knows what to them. She couldn't give in to these outrageous feelings.

Yet...

He had held her, comforted her, tended her wounds, and saved her more than once. A light beamed from his smile and sparkled in his eyes, exuding a goodness she couldn't ignore. She noted that he ensured Petunia's needs were met before his own, lit the campfires without her command, and protected her when they were in imminent danger. All these actions chipped at her staunch judgment of him.

How was it possible for someone like him to commit such a heinous crime?

Selene wasn't naive. She knew anyone could hide behind a well-crafted mask and do heinous things behind closed doors. But she sensed something more to him that didn't fit the crime he had been accused of.

Then, there were the bounty hunters to account for. They had mentioned wanting to take back what was theirs, as if the children were mere prized possessions to reclaim. Something in their tone and choice of words had made her skin crawl. They also wanted to silence her for good, ensuring they'd have no witnesses when they abducted Reid. The thought churned her stomach.

She closed her eyes as guilt nestled within her. How could she lean against him, accept his warmth, and still lead him to the Arcane Sanctum to be imprisoned for the remainder of his life?

If there was an inkling of doubt about his crimes, could she live with herself, wondering if he was an innocent man?

A heaviness settled around her heart. The sting of her past pricked her mind. She needed to escape it—to run from all these confusing feelings.

Selene pushed against Reid's arm, only for it to tighten around her. A low groan rumbled in her ear, the sound vibrating from his chest.

"Not yet," he whispered.

She tempered the rising fluttering in her stomach with a swallow.

"You're awake?" she asked, her pitch inclining.

"Shh," he said, placing a finger on her mouth. "It's not time yet."

"Reid..." She hesitated, hating the softness rounding her voice, but she couldn't bring herself to say the words. One simple command, and she'd be free of him. But all the rational thoughts vanished when his fingers curled onto the folds of her dress as if he were clinging to a precious dream.

Her breath caught in her throat, and she thanked the heavens. Her lips couldn't form words lest she say something she'd regret.

Don't let me go.

The traitorous thought echoed in her mind, but she clamped her mouth together.

"Don't ruin the dream," he murmured.

"What dream?"

"The one we'll never share if I wake up."

Selene's lips parted. Her throat tightened, and a pleasant shiver raced down her spine. Her hand hovered where his beating heart thrummed faster beneath her ear, torn between surrendering into his embrace or pushing him away.

"Then," she started before she could stop herself, "keep dreaming, Piper."

His arm flexed around her slightly, and his chin nestled against her hair. Every protocol imprinted in her screamed to cease this at once, but she ignored the voices and closed her eyes. For a moment, she could pretend they were just two people lost in the world who'd found each other...

A distressed squeak cut through the silence. Petunia chittered anxiously, rising on her hind legs, and nodded, gesturing upward to indicate something. Reid tensed beneath her. Suddenly, the security of his arms vanished, and he rose to his feet to peek through the window. Selene secretly mourned the loss of his warmth, but the fear in his eyes alarmed her.

The sound of heavy footsteps and low voices drew closer.

"...said something about heading in this direction."

"Maybe we should check inside. See if they're hiding 'round here."

Petunia skittered up Reid's leg and hid beneath his coat. He pressed a finger to his lips before nodding toward the ladder. Selene tiptoed across the loft and followed Reid down the rungs. Every step inspired nerves to explode in her stomach as she prayed the floorboards wouldn't groan beneath her.

"May I help you, gentlemen? Or do I have to escort you off my property?" another voice said. The figure's boots crunched against the gravel leading to the barn.

A weight dropped to her stomach. Reid turned to mouth the words *the farmer*, and she swallowed thickly.

"Have you seen two travelers come across this way? One male, and one female with purple hair." The deep voice belonging to the man who had nearly cleaved her in two asked—no greeting—just a cold demand.

Reid silently led her to the back door, where the voices were the furthest away. She held her breath as they passed the sheep, staring at them with unblinking eyes. They shifted in their pen, uneasy by their proximity, and Selene prayed none of them would bleat in fear.

"No, I'm afraid I haven't. I don't want any trouble here. I don't take too kindly to strangers."

"Put down the scythe, and there won't be any if you let us search your property."

The threat made her shiver. Reid gingerly opened the door without a single creak. He checked his left, right, and left again before signaling her to move. Once outside, he grabbed her hand to run toward the forest. A rapid pitter-patter sounded, and a sheen of white feathers caught the corner of her eye. Before she could warn Reid, a large goose hissed, charging at them with its neck lowered like a javelin.

"Ah, spells," he muttered.

Selene bit back a scream as the goose nipped at her skirts. A series of honks exploded from the bird. Its wings stretched out to flap aggressively at her while spearing her hem with its beak.

A hand wrapped around her arm, pulling her from the goose's reach.

Reid whirled on the bird, stomping on the ground as a threat. The goose honked louder, rearing to strike again.

"Now this—" Reid dodged left, scurrying backward. "Would be a *foul* way to die."

"Just leave it!" she said, swatting at the bird.

"What was that?" a voice in front of the barn asked.

"That's my guard goose!"

Reid huffed, taking her hand and running toward the tree line. "Of course it's a guard goose. Better defenders than dogs..."

The guard goose chased after them, alerting everyone to the intruders' escape. Once they bolted into the forest, the overgrown bird ceased its chase, but the pounding of boots followed.

Selene's heart leaped into her throat. Her hand grew slick against Reid's grasp as they ran. Leaves slapped her cheeks. Twigs crunched beneath her steps. The forest blurred like a smear of green and brown paints. Her chest ached, but the sounds of pursuit grew closer.

"Selene—" he panted. "My magic—"

A snarl ripped in his throat as he stumbled over a root. She yelped when he crashed to the ground, pulling her down with him. Suddenly, the world spun wildly, rocks and brush hitting her as they tumbled down a slope. Selene clenched her mouth shut, forcing herself to stay silent to stop a scream from escaping. At last, they came to a tangled rest, and she groaned in pain.

"You all right, Violet?" he asked, his voice tight.

"Are you?" she shot back.

"I'm—" He winced, inhaling a sharp breath. "I've been better."

Selene pushed herself from the ground, her eyes darting to every tree. She strained to hear the booming footsteps, but the sound faded. Perhaps their fall had bought them time.

When she turned, mud clung to Reid's cheek, and a twig poked out of his hair. She instinctively wiped her face, removing dirt and a few small leaves. He hissed suddenly, clutching at his ankle.

"Is it broken?" she asked hoarsely. Panic wrenched her stomach into knots.

"It's fine," he said. He wobbled to stand but collapsed to one knee with a pained grunt. "Or... perhaps less than fine."

Her pulse thundered in her ears. She glanced over her shoulder and peered up the slope. "You can't walk, can you?"

"I'll manage." But sweat dotted his brow. "There's no way a goose and spells-rotten root will best me."

His pale skin and breathless voice did not convince her. Seeing him weak and vulnerable twisted the knot in her stomach.

"Will your magic help?"

"Yes," he said. "Wild magic takes energy, especially to heal, but I'm willing to risk it."

Selene dug out his pipe from her bag. "Then use magic to heal yourself!" she ordered.

Nodding, he sat and extended his legs out. A tremor ran through his hands as he raised the pipe to his lips. A light note swirled around them, and the familiar *zing* crackled in the air. The melody carried a soft, lilting tune like a warm embrace on a frigid night. Selene stared at the injured ankle expectantly. Even with structured magic with the aid of her wand, healing was a delicate and challenging process that only few had learned to master. Even she had some difficulty setting a bone back into place. She wondered if wild magic had the same limitations—

The song warbled mid-note, producing a shrill whistle. Petunia squeaked and scurried out of Reid's coat. She then stood on her hind legs on his lap, with her ears flat against her head in worry, as Reid hissed and clamped his jaw. A muffled yell sounded behind his tight grimace.

Crack!

Selene winced, her stomach churning at the sound of bone setting. Reid moaned, his face ashen as he slumped to the ground, eyes fluttering shut. Petunia darted up his chest to touch his face with her paws. Selene's knees hit the dirt with a thud, her hands trembling and hovering above him.

"No, no, no, Reid!" she half-cried, half-whispered.

Petunia looked up at Selene, her black eyes rounded into wide saucers, squeaking sadly. Selene awkwardly cradled Reid's face, her fingers brushing aside his hair to check his pulse. It beat a slow but consistent rhythm beneath her touch.

"Reid," she tapped his face. "Please wake up!"

He didn't stir. His head lolled to the other side, and dread flattened the air from her lungs. Her head jerked at the sound of crunching detritus. Tromping footsteps echoed in the distance.

The bounty hunters were heading in her direction.

Petunia shivered, and Selene imagined the rat was sensing the imminent danger as much as she was. There wasn't much time.

Selene pushed Reid into a sitting position and hooked her arm under his. Grunting, she strained to lift him, but his weight dragged her down. Her mind raced with possible solutions before she decided to grab him by both arms to drag him away. Deep, sliding marks followed as she struggled to pull him forward. Petunia scampered behind, swiping at the visible trail with her tail to hide their tracks.

Voices could be heard a few yards away. She was going too slow for comfort. She scanned her surroundings for anything they could use to hide. Her blood pounded within her veins like the toll of a death knell with each passing second.

Petunia squeaked, darting forward. Selene's heart beat with anticipation as she followed the rat. Petunia climbed over a log, nodding and stamping her feet. Upon further inspection, Selene recognized a half-collapsed structure between some brush and fallen branches—an abandoned hunter's blind. A tattered tarp, camouflaged by the elements, was skewed atop the low frame of logs. Selene murmured a relieved prayer.

"Thank you," she said, and Petunia gave a short bow and continued to cover their tracks.

Selene ducked under the tarp and dragged Reid into the pit just as footsteps crashed into the clearing. Selene's breath stilled, her hand clamped over her mouth to silence any noise that might betray her. Her free fingers instinctively curled into Reid's shirt as she lay beside him.

A twig snapped.

"I thought they'd land here somewhere," the brunette with the axe muttered.

They drew closer, and the sound of an arrow loaded in a crossbow clicked. Selene peeked through the hidden flap where a pair of worn leather boots strode in their direction. If she didn't do something soon, they might be discovered.

Reid had said wild magic couldn't be controlled—it could only be guided. Selene didn't know what that meant, but their lives were hanging by a mere thread.

Closing her eyes, she took a deep breath before mentally plunging into her core, where her magic dwelled. Then, she extended the search further, into the essence of life pulsing through the ground and the world around her. Fire and chaotic energy bashed against her, eager to be free and reign chaos. Her first instinct was to fight it—to erect a wall to prevent it from escaping, but she stamped the urge. The energy burned, lashing against her like a firestorm until she opened her arms to embrace it.

I need your help, she cried.

She didn't resist. She didn't fight. She allowed the flood of power to consume her. Rather than being burned, coils of blazing magic wrapped around her limbs. Heat bloomed in her chest, unfurling like delicate petals. The chaos stilled, and she guided the magic to weave around her. Light bent at her gentle direction, shimmering around them until a light veil settled over the hunter's blind.

Her chest heaved. Exhaustion stole through every limb, stealing the breath from her lungs. Darkness pulled at her vision, but she fought to keep herself conscious.

The boots stopped inches before the flap.

"I thought I saw something," the brunette bounty hunter muttered.

"Well, there's nothing here. Their tracks don't lead anywhere else," another said.

"The girl is a steward. She probably used magic to escape," the third said. "They can be transported in the blink of an eye."

"Then we'd best find another trail," the brunette said.

Then, their footsteps faded into the forest.

Selene's eyes fluttered, the darkness creeping further into her mind. Petunia hopped in front of her vision, trilling and squeaking. The last thing she recalled was the rat's soft nose nuzzling her jaw before she sank into the darkness.

15

Reid woke to the scent of rain with notes of sweet lavender. Soft strands of hair tickled his cheek, and for one, foggy, blissful moment, he thought he was still dreaming in the loft of the barn with Selene in his arms. But a dull ache throbbed in his ankle, and his core was bruised and drained of all magic. Instead of wood, he shifted over a pine-needled ground with a muggy breeze blowing through his hair.

His eyes flashed open. Selene's pale face lay next to him, sweat beading at her temple, and her chest rose up and down with shallow breaths. Every muscle stiffened, his stomach coiling with dread. Reid ignored his shaky limbs as he pushed himself up.

"Selene?" he rasped.

Her lavender brows didn't twitch.

Panic raced through his thrumming pulse. The memory of being chased, tumbling down the slope, twisting his ankle before surrendering to unconsciousness, spilled in his racing mind. He reached for her, his finger grazing her cheek, but she did not stir. Reid peeked through the blind. By the sun's location in the sky, perhaps an hour had passed.

Petunia leaped into his lap, her whiskers shivering with relief as she chirped at him. Her head bobbed toward Selene, and his eyes widened.

"Of all the bold and stupid things," he muttered, his fingers brushing the strands of hair from the stewardess' face. "Why did you have to go and do something reckless like that?"

Selene had saved them, but at a cost.

Reid pulled her limp body against him, wrapping his arms around her. Wild magic wasn't something to trifle with. He'd experienced more than one occasion of passing out in dark streets when he was first learning how to guide it, and sometimes, he thought he'd never wake up from using it. There was a reason wild magic was feared, other than the chaos it could unleash.

It could also steal your life.

The dread coating his stomach thickened into a sticky pit of fear. It bubbled into nausea as he rocked Selene back and forth.

"C'mon, Violet," he murmured. "Don't let the magic take you. You're stronger than that." He pressed his forehead against her temple, his mouth lingering over the shell of her ear. Closing his eyes, his hand cradled the back of her neck.

"You're not allowed to die like this. Not before I can tell you how much of a fool I am for falling for you."

A deafening pause followed the crack of his voice. Everything stilled except the roar of his pulse rushing in his ears.

Reid supposed it was only a matter of time before he accepted the feelings for the woman who was to turn him in. It seemed only right for a villain like him to confess his feelings when Selene wasn't awake to hear them.

He shook his head with a sigh. "For better or worse, you will ruin me, but at least I'll fall with a smile."

Selene stirred, her eyes fluttering open. A mix of joy and apprehension swirled in his chest. How much had she heard of his melodramatic confession?

Her crystal eyes met his, her brows furrowing. "Reid?" she asked, her voice a rasp. "Are you all right?"

Reid chuckled. He couldn't help it. The irony of the situation couldn't be more amusing.

"Shouldn't I be asking you that?" he asked in return. "You're the one who used wild magic for the first time and knocked yourself unconscious. Don't you know how dangerous that could have been? You could have died."

"I would have died regardless of whether the bounty hunters caught us. At least I'd have a choice in the matter."

Reid frowned, the rush of panic over her well-being had yet to settle. "I know. I am both grateful and worried, but for a moment I thought..."

He shook his head, thinking better of it.

"What?" she asked.

"It doesn't matter."

"It does," she said, "Because I was scared too. You overextended yourself, and I thought I'd lost you."

Their eyes met. Reid's breath caught in his throat as his fingers instinctively gripped the blue silk of her dress.

Her eyes widened, and a red flush spread across her cheeks when her gaze dropped to his arms around her, as if realizing their closeness. Her lips parted, and her eyes flickered with hesitation. His heart pounded like a hammer against his ribs, wondering if she'd stay or tear herself away from him.

In the end, she removed herself from his grasp. Disappointment speared through him, but he hid it with an easy smile.

"We should probably start heading out," she said, folding her arms tight around her chest.

Reid shot her a pointed look. "And how exactly will you travel after spending all your energy?"

She pressed her lips together, then said. "We can't just sit here while they're after us. They could backtrack to our location at any time. Besides, you passed out, too. How should my situation be any different?"

"Because I've had more experience recovering from these magic stunts. It doesn't take me nearly as long to regain my strength. But you?" He eyed her up and down. "It might take an hour or two before you can wobble like a newborn fawn."

Selene pursed her lips with a glint of defiance in her eyes. She crawled out of the hovel on shaky limbs. She attempted to stand once, twice, and then three times, but fell flat on her face each time. Reid bit back a smirk as he leaned nonchalantly against a tree. Petunia scurried beside him and stood on her hind legs, mimicking him.

"Shut up," she snapped.

"I didn't say anything."

"I can tell you're mocking me in your head. Both of you."

Reid glanced at Petunia and shrugged. She gave a slight shrug of her own. "Are you done? Because, like you said, we need to move."

"But how—"

Before she could protest, Reid bent down and scooped her up into his arms. Selene squealed, squirming against his chest.

"What are you doing?" she demanded, her face flushing.

"Carrying you. What does it look like?"

"You can't carry me!"

A sharp zing stung his throat, but he did not drop her. He raised an eyebrow. "Is that an order? Because you can crawl there if you'd like."

Huffing in annoyance, she crossed her arms.

"Fine," she grumbled. "Carry me. But I don't like it."

Reid couldn't help but chuckle. "Noted."

She shot him a glare but said nothing more. Petunia's amused squeaks followed him before she scampered ahead to scout for any dangers lurking on the road.

Wet leaves squelched beneath his boots, and puddles mirrored the beads of water dripping from leaves. The scent of petrichor, damp bark, and moss clung to the air as he traveled. After walking for a while, he spoke to fill the silence.

"You know, I've been thinking a lot about what's gonna happen when we get to the Arcane Sanctum."

She glanced up at him with a frown.

"When we reach the Stewards," he continued, his voice quiet. "What are you going to do? Is turning me in gonna fix whatever you did?"

Selene stiffened in his arms. "I-I have to. It's my atonement."

Reid considered her words carefully. "You must have broken a serious rule if they want you to trade my life for your reputation."

Her jaw tightened.

"Let me guess," he began lightly. "A spell went wrong? Or did you insult the wrong High Steward?"

"Stop it, Reid. I don't want to play this game with you."

"C'mon, it couldn't have been that serious. It's not like you cursed someone, right?" he asked jokingly.

Selene's cheeks flushed, and she looked away.

A spell of silence thickened the air. Reid blinked, his mind scrambling to make sense of her hesitation. Surely, she would deny such a terrible accusation? Still, she remained silent.

The steady beat of his heart slowed until it dropped to the pit of his stomach. Quietly, he placed her on a nearby log and took a step back. She still couldn't look him in the eye.

His grandmother used to read him stories about heroes of old, and their noble quests to save the world from evil. Some were about stewards battling against a curse an evil arcanist placed upon the kingdom. Another was about a prince who climbed the highest tower to wake a princess from a sleeping curse that had been bestowed upon her by a bitter stewardess. In every story, the moral was the same: Good triumphs over evil, but every curse leaves a scar.

"I was only jesting—you couldn't possibly have—"

His breath caught short when she shifted away from him.

The puzzle pieces clicked into place—why she'd been so determined to hunt him down. If she failed this, her whole life as she knew it would end if she didn't atone for what she had done.

And she had the nerve to call *him* the villain.

Suddenly, he couldn't recognize the woman before him. The world tilted beneath his boots as a pressure built behind his eyes.

"That doesn't seem characteristic of you, Violet," he murmured.

"And what would you know about me?" she snapped. "You know nothing."

"I guess you're right. I don't know you after all." He said, taking a step closer. A flash of sorrow lit her eyes before they dropped to her lap as if the fabric there was most interesting. Reid continued, "Tell me why the righteous stewardess would curse someone? What did they do to deserve it?"

Her hands curled into fists. "I...It was deserved."

"Was it?" he challenged.

"I don't need to explain myself."

Reid scoffed. "I think you owe me the courtesy as your captive who has willingly carried you toward my prison. They're about to lock the key, throw it away, and let me rot in a cell for the rest of my life. Yet, here I am, a fool who's happy to be led by your chain."

A long pause followed, and then Selene sighed. "The prince was out of control."

His brows raised to his forehead. Of all the people to curse, royalty was one of the worst offenses. Selene dove into her tale, explaining how she was tasked to be one of his advisors, the untimely death of the king and queen, and the subsequent abuse that followed at the prince's hands. Then she disguised herself as a beggar woman and offered the prince a rose as his last chance of redemption. When rejected, she cursed him into a beast, transforming the rest of his court into walking, talking puppets—just as the prince treated them.

"Are you satisfied?" she finished with a scowl.

His chest tightened. Rage flickered beneath the surface as he stared long and hard at her.

"I don't believe it."

Her eyes snapped up at him. "What?"

Reid expelled a bitter sigh. "You heard me. Your story is too convoluted—too clean. The truth is usually much simpler."

Her pretty lashes fluttered incredulously at him. "I don't know what you're insinuating—!"

"I think it's pretty clear what I'm insinuating," he said, folding his arms tight across his chest. "You're a terrible liar, Violet."

Selene flinched, her voice becoming shrill. "I'm not lying!"

"Don't insult me," he spat. "I've had enough experience with people deceiving me to know a bold-faced lie when I hear one. The only question I have for you is: Why? What are you hiding?" He hunched his shoulders in question.

"I'm not—"

In three steps, he closed the distance between them. He knelt before her, leaning in so their faces were inches apart. She shrank from his proximity. Her blue eyes darted away.

"Then why won't you look me in the eye, Violet?"

16

There were a thousand clever lies on the tip of Selene's tongue. She could have crafted another tale that would keep her dignity intact—one where she was still the hero of her story. But the hurt in Reid's blazing, amber eyes cut through each one before she could voice them.

Somehow, he'd learned to see past the walls she had painstakingly built around her heart. She was forged in the fires of rigidity, where no mistakes were tolerated. Perfectionism was to be achieved at any cost, even if that meant lying through her teeth.

When the High Stewards had brought her to be judged, she couldn't control the truths they already knew, but she could twist them into a tale of heroism to save herself from the undeniable shame.

If she were going to fall into disgrace, she would fall with the least amount of casualties to her name.

But the truth was uglier. She brushed it under some dainty rug in the recesses of her mind, never to be looked at again. It was easier to pretend she was the pious stewardess her father raised her to be.

Now, Reid made it impossible to keep up the charade.

Selene swallowed thickly at how close he was—how his eyes searched her soul for the truth. Tension crackled in the air like lightning before it strikes. Perhaps he deserved to know after everything he'd done for her.

However, a small voice whispered he'd never look at her with the same softness as this morning. He wouldn't want to brush hands when he thought she wasn't looking, or hold her in his arms if another storm rolled in. All the moments she secretly treasured would come to an end.

Perhaps it was for the best. Whatever *this* was between them would never see a happily ever after.

Finally, she met his expectant gaze. A tremble ran through her spine. "Because the truth destroys what little dignity I have."

The hard glint of his eyes softened. Backing away, Reid sat back on his heels, and she expelled the breath she'd been holding.

"Dignity?" he began in a light, teasing tone. "I've slept on the streets and played with rats. I don't think I have a shred of dignity left. What I care about is the truth. I'd rather see all your broken, honest parts than the perfect lie you serve to the world. Let me see *you*."

Selene's pulse thrummed beneath her skin. A hot wave of emotion pricked at her eyes, clenching her throat in a vice grip. She didn't dare speak lest her voice crack with tears. Her nose burned, but she swallowed the stinging sensations down. Someone wanted to see her for who she truly was, but that scared her more than banishment ever could.

"You won't like what you see," she sniffed.

A small, crooked smile rose on his lips. "Let me be the judge of that."

Her muscles quivered like gelatin. She was still too weak from expending wild magic and couldn't run away even if she wanted to. There was nowhere to hide. And for the first time, she didn't want to.

Selene gathered the dregs of her courage and sighed. "I didn't secure a seat as a High Steward. Father was livid. It was everything he had prepared me for my whole life, and I failed. He screamed at me, saying how much of a disappointment I was. But then, the High Stewards sent me to Evarandor as a stewardess in service of the royal family. My father assigned me one last task," she said, grimacing. "He wanted me to seduce the prince."

Selene shook her head, hoping to stamp down the rising emotions that were swallowing her whole.

"Becoming a future queen was the next best honor for our family," she continued. "If I failed, I would disgrace my father. But wooing the prince was not as easy as my father or I assumed it would be. Prince Leander had no interest in me and..."

Selene paused to take control of the quiver in her voice. "I couldn't stand the rejection. How could he not want me? I'm beautiful and powerful... but I wasn't enough for him. I *failed* the second task my father gave me—the only chance I had left to prove myself worthy. To finally earn his love—" her voice cracked, and a breath hitched in her throat when a gentle thumb wiped a tear from her cheek.

Selene didn't know when he'd stood, crossed the distance between them, and sat beside her. Crocodile tears streamed down her face in fast rivulets, and her chest heaved.

The words barely escaped past her shuddering sob. "All my life, I worked and I worked to please my father. For once in my life, I just wanted to feel like he loved me."

Selene buried her face in her hands. The tears exploded from her chest like too much pressure in a potion flask. Reid rubbed a hand up and down her back in soothing motions.

At last, she found her voice again. "Prince Leander's rejection provoked something in me—something dark and ugly. I was enraged, hurt, and frightened. I wanted him to feel my pain. In my anger, I cursed him into a beast. Only true love would be able to break it. If he couldn't love me, then I would make it impossible for anyone else to love him. And I would create a story that would justify my actions..." she trailed off, her voice waning.

Selene sniffed and looked up at the treetops. "I thought if I told the right story, I would be praised as a hero for stopping a prince who was out of control," another humorless laugh escaped her. "I suppose that proves I was a bigger fool than I thought. My father was right about me."

"Right about what?"

"How much of a disappointment I am. I proved I was the mess-up he always thought me to be."

Reid was silent longer than was comfortable, but his thumb continued to wipe away the stray tears.

"I don't think you failed, Violet. I think your father failed *you*," he said softly.

"No... it was all me," she said, dropping her gaze into her lap. "I failed over and over again."

"Look at me, Violet," Reid said gently. A finger coaxed her chin up, and she swallowed the knot in her throat when their eyes met.

"I meant that your father doesn't have to define who you are. You are not the broken, unlovable woman you believe you are. I've seen your determination. I see the goodness within you. You are more than what that spells-awful man of a father says of you."

Her eyes prickled, and more tears silently spilled down her cheeks. "He's not awful... he's just strict," she said, but the words faltered on her tongue. She didn't know why she was defending her father. The truth of what Reid said struck her like a boulder flung by a trebuchet.

"I know he's your father, but listen to me," he said, cradling her wet cheek in his palm. "No good man who calls himself a father would treat their daughter this way. The pressure he puts on you is too great for one person to bear. I understand the emotions behind why you would snap after being treated that way all your life. The prince didn't deserve to be cursed... but he must also be blind to miss what a rare gem you are. You have wildfire in your veins with the beauty of the stars. It's not your fault he couldn't see that."

Selene's swollen eyes widened, and the raw ache of her emotions suddenly quieted. The heat of his hand on her cheek and the softness of his gaze nearly undid her. It was a quiet, gentle look with unspoken words she could sense between them. *You're not alone. I'm here.*

For the first time, someone saw *her*. Reid did not condone her actions, but he saw the pain, the endless chase of approval, and the loneliness buried in her heart.

Another wave of tears caught her off guard.

The prince didn't deserve to be cursed.

Her throat clenched. Instinctively, she leaned forward, resting her forehead against his shoulder. She couldn't speak even if she wanted to. Her cries wrenched from a deep place she never thought would see the light of day.

Reid's hand stroked her back softly. Between her sobs, the wind pushing through the trees, and the birds continuing their songs, Reid's silence comforted her the most.

A skittering noise sounded. Selene raised her head as Petunia darted toward them, kicking dirt and leaves up in her path. She squeaked and jumped onto Reid in a graceful leap. Her nose twitched in agitation as she jerked her head back.

Reid's shoulders stiffened, his head snapping up.

Something whined in the air. In a flash, Reid wrapped his arms around her, pulling her to the ground. The air knocked from her chest, her skull rattling when it crashed onto the forest floor. An arrow struck into the log where she had just been sitting.

Reid spun around, blocking her with his body.

Three men came out of the trees, weapons drawn. The bounty hunter with the axe grinned with glee as he approached. Soon, they were only a few feet away. "See?

I told you I spotted something back here. Thought you could keep running, Piper?"

"You guys are sure slow," Reid said with an air of nonchalance. He took a step forward, still blocking her view of the threatening men. "Considering I'm carrying a wounded woman. Kinda embarrassing, really."

The axe-wielder lunged at him. Selene held back a scream as Reid dodged, weaving around his attacks with practiced ease.

"C'mon, you could at least give us the decency to state why you're after us," Reid said, side-stepping another blow.

From the corner of her eye, the black-haired man aimed his crossbow at her. She clawed the ground, hoping to get enough traction, but her body wouldn't move. Her limbs were heavy as lead.

The crossbow clicked, but the man let out a high-pitched yelp. The arrow shot somewhere left as he hopped on one foot, shaking the other leg. He screamed in pain as a small lump moved its way up his pants and into his tunic.

"Get it out!" he yelled. "Get this thing out!"

Petunia's head popped from his collar before biting him in the neck. Another pained cry wrenched from the man's throat, causing the crossbow to fall to the ground with a thud.

Selene used this distraction to reach for her bag. Sweat beads formed on her forehead as her arms strained to grab it. Reid ducked and feinted left when the third bounty hunter swung his sword. The two men were cornering him toward a tree. Soon, he wouldn't have anywhere to run.

Her fingertips finally touched the straps of her bag and pulled it toward her to rummage inside.

"Reid!" she cried out, whipping out his pipe. "Use your magic!"

Selene threw the instrument, hoping and praying she had the strength to make the distance. Reid caught it effortlessly. The axe-man thrust the blunt side of his weapon at Reid's head, but it struck the tree when he ducked.

Soft, eerie notes resonated from the pipe. An electrifying spark charged in the air, its power tingling down her spine. Reid's fingers flew over his instrument, weaving a hypnotic song. The three bounty hunters froze, their weapons suspended in mid-air. The crossbow man fell over, losing his balance on one foot, and remained motionless in the same position. They were locked in time—only their eyes moved back and forth in alarm.

Reid glanced up at her, his gesture clearly conveying his message. Selene recognized the magic of influence in the men's stances. Their defenses were down, making them more susceptible to her sway. She sat up straighter and cleared her throat. Reid couldn't stop playing, or else the spell would break, but all her commands would remain effective long after his music ended.

"You three," she called out, "turn toward me."

On command, they slowly pivoted, even the man on the ground, shuffled to face her.

"You with the axe," she addressed the brunette man. "Who sent you?"

The man's expression turned slack, his eyes glazing. "The mayor of Hamlin."

Selene's eyes rounded. "The mayor? Why would he want me dead?"

"He told us not to leave any witnesses," the man droned.

Selene's stomach dropped. "Do you know where the children are?"

"We found a lead. Other men are tracking them as we speak. Up north in the Glimmerwild."

A note cracked a piercing sound. Something flashed in Reid's eyes—a look of panic. Sweat gleamed off his forehead, and his shoulders slumped. Selene swallowed thickly. He was running low on energy again.

"What does the mayor want with Reid if you're close to finding the children?"

"Revenge."

"And what does the mayor want with the children?"

"He wants what we want—our property back."

Something cold and furious coiled in Selene's chest. Another discordant note broke from the pipe, and she grimaced. They were out of time.

"Leave us and don't pursue us again," she said. "Go as far south as you possibly can—walk, go by boat, or by whatever means necessary. Now."

The men marched off, and when they were out of sight, Reid gasped. The flute thudded to the ground, and he fell to his knees, panting. Selene sat helplessly, but one question burned at the tip of her tongue.

"What did they mean?"

Reid glanced at her, his body trembling. "I suppose... It's time I tell you the truth."

17

A tremble ran through Reid's spine as he sat across from Selene. The wind whistled through the trees as the mist evaporated under the sun. Within a few short hours, so much had changed—something had shifted between them. Whatever bridge they crossed, they couldn't turn back now.

Reid pushed a hand through his hair and sighed. Selene's expectant stare bored a hole through his skull, but he wasn't sure where to start. Petunia crawled up his vest, sat on his shoulder, and put one little paw on his cheek as if to encourage him to speak the truth and shed his mask.

"Yeah, I know it's about time," he muttered to Petunia. He cast his gaze on Selene. Her red-rimmed, blue eyes were swollen, the tip of her nose red, and tear tracks carved down her face. She had told him the harsh truth of her past actions, and he figured he owed her the same courtesy—not to win her trust, but because, for once, he wanted to be truthful.

"I never thought I'd tell you about any of this, to be honest," he started. "I didn't trust you."

"I suppose that's fair. I didn't trust you either," she said.

He hesitated, his mouth pressing into a thin line. "It all started with a steward. I learned not to trust them."

Selene frowned. "What do you mean?"

Memories of the past echoed within him, the pain reverberating against the hollow of his chest. He had shared the story with only two creatures, Petunia included, and this was the first time he would tell the tale to another human.

"I'll start with this: The children are not safe in the village of Hamlin. Those people there are not their parents. They've been stolen away and used to mine an energy source."

Selene stiffened, but she didn't interrupt him.

"It's called feralite," he said, his voice lowering. "It's being cultivated for the masses so that non-magical people may be able to wield magic as if they were well-seasoned stewards."

Selene's mouth parted. "Feralite? But that's not possible. It's illegal. Something that powerful would only bring chaos."

Reid nodded grimly. "Yes. The one behind it all is a steward. I don't know his name otherwise. They only call him by his title."

Selene shook her head as though trying to make sense of it. "And children are being forced to mine it?"

"Yes." Reid's jaw clenched under the weight of the memories continuing to haunt him. "Children are the only ones who can mine Feralite. The steward figured out that their untapped magic and potential don't react to the raw and unstable crystal the way adults do."

"Because they'll go mad," Selene whispered. "Or it'll kill them."

Reid nodded. "Even if they successfully refine the Feralite, the wild magic from it will only destroy people."

Selene stared at him, her expression unsure. He wouldn't blame her if she didn't believe him. It was a truth too devious to believe.

"How do you know all this?" she asked, her brows furrowing.

Reid swallowed. His mouth wouldn't form the words. Petunia nudged him gently with her soft muzzle, and he petted her to soothe the monsters of his past from swallowing him whole.

At last, he forced himself to speak.

"Because I was one of them."

She blinked slowly. "One of... who?"

"A child who was taken."

Reid took a deep breath. He paused, allowing time for the rising emotions to settle in the silence. The day he'd been taken and forced into chains remained stitched on his heart. But the days, months, and years following were a nightmare, submerged in murky water, and he didn't know if he could call it a blessing or a curse that he couldn't remember much.

A squirrel skittered up a tree, grounding him to reality and the woman who sat patiently for the rest of his story.

"It happened two years after my grandmother passed. I'd been living on the streets and was easy pickings. They can detect which children have the potential for magic, and it's easy to lure anyone hungry enough to follow you into a covered wagon," he huffed a wry chuckle. "Next thing I know, I'm blindfolded, chained, and thrown in a dark cavern with about a hundred other children. The rest is a blur, but it wasn't pretty. The only one who kept me sane was Tomas, a boy younger than me. He'd sing songs to cheer me up, and taught me how to whistle."

The image of a freckled, brunette eight-year-old with a gap between his front top teeth surfaced. All the days and nights he spent with Tomas, and the jokes and songs they shared to pass the darkest moments, panged in his chest.

"Tomas and I wanted to escape and eventually find a way to free all the children. A storm rolled in, and one of the shafts collapsed. Thankfully, no one was hurt, but there was an opening on the other side. Tomas pushed me through to run and escape before the guards came back. Only one of us could squirm through before more of it collapsed on us. I promised I would return for him—" Reid's voice faltered, the image of Tomas' reassuring smile still plagued his dreams.

He pushed himself to continue. "Once I got out, I ran and ran as far as I could. I tried to tell the sheriff of the nearest town what was happening, but no one believed me. By the time I returned to save Tomas... there was nothing there. They must have packed up when they were one child short and moved to another area to mine. Ever since, I haven't stopped looking."

Petunia nuzzled his jaw again, and he glanced at his trembling hands. "But I finally found them," he said. "I found the children... but I couldn't find Tomas. He would be around my age now, but... I can't help but feel like I failed him."

A cool hand rested on his own. He glanced up at Selene's face, her eyes glistening, and he shook his head.

"They're safe now, though," he said. "The children are safe."

"How did you get them out?" she asked cautiously.

Reid shoved his hands into his pockets. "I stole them away. In the middle of the night, I loosened their bonds, made everyone sleep, and had the kids follow me out of their quarters. Performing such magic nearly killed me. It's difficult to influence one person, let alone twenty guards stationed by the mines. I led them to Glimmerwood forest and entrusted their safety to someone I trust. I've been trying to keep the bounty hunters on my trail, hoping they wouldn't find them."

"What if they find the children?" she asked.

His lips curled. "If what they said is true, then I have to go back and make sure they're safe."

Selene grabbed his arm. "What if that's exactly what they want you to do? To go back to them?"

He took a deep breath, his jaw clenched. "Then it's a risk I'm willing to take. I can't risk the alternative. If I don't do anything and they find them... I will never be able to live with myself."

"Can't you message the person who's taking care of them?"

Reid shook his head. "No. They're a wood sprite. There's no way to contact them."

Selene blinked rapidly, and Reid couldn't say he blamed her. Not many humans had ever had contact with wood sprites, but this one had helped care for him after he had scared off some hunters who were being cruel to a squirrel on his travels.

For a moment, her silence inspired knots to tangle in his stomach. Reid didn't know if she believed his story or if she would allow him to save the children. She could easily order him to keep moving to the Arcane Sanctum to face his trial.

At last, she locked eyes with him. "What do you suppose we do, then?"

18

Selene's skin prickled, her heart stuttering with the undeniable truths. Everything she knew about the man before her had shattered and been pieced back together within the same breath.

All her doubts about his criminal past proved her intuition to be true. Reid was not the villain she had thought. The High Stewards were wrong.

Her thoughts reeled. What else had she been told wasn't true? Who among the Arcane Stewards could she trust? Reid had said a steward was leading the vile operation, but who else could be involved? Surely not every steward or stewardess was guilty?

Selene's mind raced with the possibility. The High Stewards would never do anything this foul, she was sure of it, but Selene had also been sure Reid was a villain deserving of imprisonment. Perhaps there was only one steward to blame, whoever they were. If that was the case, she needed to inform the one person she *did* trust:

Lysandriel, the Supreme High Steward.

Reid stared at her, his shoulders heavy and his eyes burdened with the weight of his past he'd confessed to her. He reached for her hand, relief softening his expression, but his fingers shook. "We must go back and save them."

Selene frowned, her eyes searching the forest floor as if it would bring her counsel. The muggy breeze disturbed her hair covered in grime, and the leaves whistled in her silence.

"What is your plan? You can't just say *save them* without a plan."

Reid rubbed the back of his neck. "I don't have a formal plan yet. All I know is that I must go before they're discovered."

"You need to think about this," she said, reaching for his arm. Her legs were still useless, but she pulled herself close to grab his sleeve. "You can't just charge in without backup. How are you going to transport more than a hundred children on your own?"

"I'll take them to the mountains if I have to," Reid replied, his voice tight. He ran a hand through his hair, a frown on his lips. A few strands fell across his furrowed brow. "I don't know... I don't know if the bounty hunters are already there. I need to go now."

Reid shifted to stand, but Selene's hand gripped tighter. "You can't just rush in when it could be a trap. We need help."

"Who will help us? I don't have time to argue about this. I have to go!" He jerked his arm and stood over her.

A metallic taste of fear filled her mouth as she peered helplessly up at him. Was he going to leave her?

"You can't," she said, attempting to steady her fluttering heart. He stiffened, his face paling as a hum of magic electrified the air. Her eyes darted to the collar, and she hesitated, her gaze dropping to the leaves scattered on the ground. "Please, Reid, I want to save them too. But we can't do this recklessly."

His hands clenched into fists until his knuckles whitened. "There is no time for that."

Selene scooted closer, dragging mud across her skirts. Desperation sank its claws into her heart as her mind raced.

"Maybe we can go to the High Stewards," she suggested.

"The High Stewards?" Reid scoffed a bitter sound that echoed through the trees. "You think they're going to help me? Believe me? One of them is behind all of this. They're not going to listen, and you know it."

"I refuse to believe *all* of them are behind this. There's a chance they might listen to me—"

"You can stay naive all you want, but I don't have time for this." His eyes narrowed on her with his jaw set. "Are you going to command me not to go? Are you going to stop me?"

Selene swallowed, hating how his eyes hardened—how hurt and betrayal dipped in his voice.

"I..." she broke off, and her stomach curled. "I know what's at stake, and I know the children are in danger. But I feel like you're heading into a trap—"

Reid curled his fists tighter. "I cannot let these children go back. If you take me to the Stewards, I will never see the light of day again. They will never believe me." His voice cracked, raw with panic and anger.

"You don't know that," she whispered.

"Please, Selene. Please don't do this to me. Don't do this to the children."

Selene swallowed hard. It was the first time he had used her name. Of all the ways she imagined him saying it, she hoped it would be in a moment of tenderness. Her heart ached.

Two choices lay before her. She could go with him to save the children, perhaps fall for the bounty hunter's trap, or be found trying to save the children. They didn't know how many men would be waiting, or if the bounty hunters would track them down while they traveled with over a hundred vulnerable children. She would not be able to use the full force of her magic, and Reid would be forced to fight on his own.

Or, she could force him to the Arcane Sanctum. She could convince the High Stewards of his innocence, have her wand and magic restored, and perhaps an army of stewards to rescue the children if they believed and trusted her. However, if Reid was right, the High Stewards might still throw him in prison, and she would never see him again. The children would be taken, and Reid would despise her for the rest of his life.

Selene tensed, sensing the sands of time slipping from her fingers as he stared at her pleadingly. There had to be another way—some other solution she hadn't thought of. But his expectant gaze and the ominous, devastating consequences of each path paralyzed her.

Petunia padded toward her and stopped inches from her knee. The little rat placed a paw on her leg, her whiskers quivering. Although Selene could not decipher the speech of rodents, she understood the imploring look in her beady, black eyes. Selene sighed and, for the first time, petted Petunia on her head. The golden fur was softer than she expected, and Petunia leaned into her touch.

Selene's heart lurched. Another path—a different choice suddenly became clear to her. She peered up at Reid, her pulse thundering like the storm last evening. The night when everything changed. Since then, she knew.

She could never turn him in.

Selene crawled even closer to him, grateful for the little energy pouring into her stiff limbs. Only an hour ago, she had woken beside him, and he'd carried her like she was something to be treasured. How had her whole world tumbled upside down in such a short amount of time? The raw ache of her confession still burned, the biting fear for her life when the bounty hunters had returned lingered, but the truths of Reid's story left no room for doubt. Everything would change, here and now.

She gestured for him to kneel next to her. He obeyed, and as soon as his knees hit the ground, her hands rose to his neck. Reid's eyes flicked to her lips, before they stared back at her, soft and surprised. Shivers danced down the length of her spine, but she remained focused. Her fingers fell over the collar, the metal cool beneath her touch. A click echoed between them. The collar fell.

Reid's eyes widened. "What...?"

"You're free now," she whispered.

A slight tremble ran through his hands as he reached for his bare neck. The knob at his throat bobbed, and a mixture of relief, shock, and something raw flashed in his gaze.

"I'm... free?"

"Yes," she nodded, and tears pressed against her eyes. "You're free."

Perhaps she was throwing away her opportunity to retrieve her wand, her reputation, and her parents' approval, but she never felt freer.

He leaned forward, wrapping his hands around hers like a prayer. "Then you're coming with me?"

She slowly shook her head. "I can't."

The hopeful glint in his eyes dimmed, and she cursed herself. "Why?"

"Because... I must return to the Arcane Sanctum."

Reid's jaw clenched, his eyes darkening like a storm. "So, you're still hoping to convince them? Or is this about your so-called 'atonement'?"

"That's not what this is about!" she cried. "We need all the help we can get. We cannot do this alone."

"Yes, we can. We have survived everything that's come our way," he said, "We can do anything."

Her heart stuttered. After everything she had done, he still wished to be by her side. Her throat squeezed, and her stomach twisted. She didn't deserve someone like him.

"Look at me, you can't keep carrying me," she said, gesturing to her useless legs. "I'll slow you down."

"That's not stopped me before."

"I need my wand," she pressed. "I can save you and all the children at my full strength. I won't be useless." She hung her head, ashamed. Up until now, she'd only been a burden without her magic. Reid had saved her more times than she wished to admit, but she was done being saved. For once, it was her turn.

He frowned. "You are more than your magic, Selene. Your worth is not tied to how useful you are or how you can benefit someone else. You have never been a burden to me."

Tears slipped down her face. For years, she had been taught the opposite. She was only good enough if she achieved her father's goals and was of use to him. Reid's words unearthed another wound deep within her, but she couldn't believe him.

"I have to go back."

His shoulders sagged. "Then I'll have to go without you."

Selene didn't trust her voice. The familiar sting of tears seared her throat as she shook her head.

Reid stood, and Petunia climbed his pant leg and perched on his shoulder. "Are you sure this is what you want?"

"Yes," she said, her voice a mere rasp.

"Then... I suppose this is goodbye. Thank you." A pause followed, and something vulnerable dipped in his voice. "I don't know if we will meet again."

"We will," she reassured him. "I'm coming back for you, Reid."

She would die trying if she must.

He took a deep breath. "The children are beneath the old, abandoned monastery, deep in the Glimmerwood forest by the river bend. But by the time you reach me, we'll probably be gone, or you can assume the worst has happened."

Her heart seized. "Reid, don't—promise me you'll be safe. Please."

A wry smile tugged on his lips. "No promises."

Before he turned, his gaze lingered—something unspoken written in his deep, amber eyes. Then, he slung his bag over his shoulder, pipe in hand, and disappeared into the trees.

Selene strained to follow his silhouette, but when she lost sight of him, her chest heaved. She didn't know if she had made another catastrophic mistake, but she wasn't going to let it stop her from finding him again.

19

R eid's heart beat in sync with the seconds ticking against him. A thousand questions consumed his thoughts.

What if the bounty hunters had found the children first? What if he could never find the children again? What if they were hurt all because of him?

And... what if he never saw Selene again?

Reid pushed himself to move faster than he ever had before, letting a drip of magic power his steps. He couldn't allow the last thought to distract him, but a raw ache settled deep in his gut. It curled around his ribs and choked the breath from his throat.

She set him free.

Although he had spent weeks attempting to manipulate her, he couldn't believe she had released him from the collar. Why had she done it? It was what he had wanted, yet pain refused to dislodge itself from his core.

Selene chose not to follow him. Instead, she foolishly believed she could convince the high and mighty stewards to aid the infamous Pied Piper. Even if she managed to persuade them of his innocence, he feared it would be too late. Action must be taken. He could not spare a moment longer.

So why was he tempted to turn around and run back to the stewardess?

The expanse of trees was too quiet, too empty without her presence. Or perhaps, he realized, she took up more space in his head than he thought. From the moment he saw her push through the crowd, her glare as sharp as ice, and her determined scowl perched on her pink lips, he knew he was done for. The stewardess not only managed to apprehend him, but she also single-hand-edly captured his heart.

Now she was gone. If he somehow managed to live through all this, he prayed he could see her one last time.

The wind seemed to bend to his will as he ran in a fraction of the time it would typically take. Wild magic coursed through his body, giving strength to his muscles while slowly depleting his stores of energy. His heart hammered with urgency, and each breath burned in his lungs.

The familiar darkness crept around his vision. If he used too much wild magic, he'd render himself useless, but the moment he slowed down, he knew he'd never forgive himself. Petunia shivered beneath his coat as she clung to his vest. Fear vibrated from her little body—fear for *him*—yet, he could not pause to reassure her.

Too much was at stake. Too many children were on the line. He needed to push himself even faster.

The path to the monastery was familiar to him, even though it was hidden behind dense foliage and twisting vines. Man long forgot the ancient underground fortress, but the forest remembered. He slipped through a narrow crack between two large boulders, ducking under hanging vines and stepping into the concealed entrance.

Reid knocked on the wooden door three times, tapped it twice, and blew a soft note from his pipe. After a moment, a small, camouflaged panel in the door opened. Bright green eyes peered out, lighting up in recognition.

"Reid!" The door swung open, revealing Fig—a wood sprite with bark-like skin and mossy hair trailing down her back. She was shorter, reaching his waist, and moved with a grace that belied her age and the thick vines that made up her limbs.

He barely had time to breathe before she wrapped him in a vine-filled hug, her wooden fingers curling around his arm.

"Reid!"

Echoes of small voices rang through the crumbling hall. Several children emerged from various nooks and crannies and raced toward him. More arms wrapped around his waist, and some around his legs.

"Where were you?" a little girl cried out.

"We missed you!"

"Don't leave us again!"

Reid smiled softly at the children tugging at his clothes. "I'm sorry, everyone. I had to make sure they wouldn't find you."

"You've been gone longer than you said you would," Fig said, a hint of worry in her bright eyes. "I thought the worst had happened."

Reid sighed and lowered his voice. "Unfortunately, you're not far from the truth. We don't have much time. The bounty hunters—"

She immediately sobered. "They've discovered us?" she whispered.

He nodded grimly. "They said they've found our trail. We have to move them—now."

Fig's face hardened, and she pulled back, ushering the children to move. "Gather your things, little ones! Quickly now!"

The silence burst with sound and movement. Suddenly, all the arms around him vanished. Some of the older children took the younger ones by the hand. The youngest of them sniffled and whined. Guilt panged in Reid's heart. They had been safe here, laughing, playing hide and seek, and chasing each other just as children were meant to do. It hurt to know he had to tear them from this small sanctuary.

"What do we do, Fig?" Reid asked, running his hands through his hair. "If they're already on their way, we might not have time to get to the mountains."

She pursed her lips, her face creasing with worry. "There are mountain sprites farther north. If you explain the situation, they might take the children in. They're more territorial than I am, and they know how to conceal their presence. But if you give them this—" Fig plucked a flower from her shoulder and handed it to him. "Then they'll know I sent you."

Reid admired the soft purple petals and frowned. "Can't you come with us?"

Fig gave him a sad, knowing smile. "You know I'm bound to the forest. I can't go beyond the trees. I'll protect the entrance as long as I can, but you'll need to move fast."

"Fast where?"

Reid turned to face an orange-haired young girl about eight years old. Her wide, green eyes glistened as she peered up at him.

Reid knelt before her, and soon, a dozen other children with their small packs crowded around him again. "To the mountains. We'll find another safe place for you there, I promise."

"I like it here, though," a ten-year-old boy said as he clung to Fig's arm.

"I know you do," Reid said apologetically, "But it's not safe anymore—"

A scream shattered through the air. The children froze, some whimpering as he bolted toward the sound, his heart in his throat. Toward the back of the hall, a large man snatched a child by the back of his shirt. Some children on the second floor threw rocks and sticks at the assailant, trying to free their friend.

Twenty more men flooded into the room from the back door. Reid reached for his pipe, but just as he lifted it to his lips, someone tackled him from behind, pinning his arms to his sides. Fig sprang into action, her vine-like limbs lashing out at the attackers. Reid kicked and threw his head back to hit the man's teeth. In a breathless swoop, the air flattened from Reid's chest. His face hit stone, and the world erupted into a dizzying swirl of colors. The man's weight crushed him to the ground. Screams echoed around him. Vague, large shapes grabbed the running children.

Vines shot out in each direction. They cracked like whips flaying hide. From his peripheral vision, Fig managed to trip five of the men and yank another to the ground, but before she could do more, strong arms wrapped around her middle. Another man appeared with a torch, holding it dangerously close to her face.

"No!" Reid struggled against his captor, but the man twisted his arm painfully behind his back. Fig froze, her eyes wide with fear as the flames licked her moss-covered hair.

The man with the torch sneered at Reid. "We've been looking for you, Piper."

Reid growled, straining against the man on top of him. "Let the children go, you spell-rotten cretins!"

"They're our property. You had no right to take them, Piper," the deep voice cut through the chaos, and Mayor Hamlin stepped into the empty hall with a smug smile.

"They're not yours," Reid hissed. "They don't belong to you!"

Mayor Hamlin shrugged. "It's not my problem how they got here. The benefactor pays well, and they're good little workers. No one will miss them."

Reid's blood boiled. "You're a monster."

The mayor ignored him, giving a signal to the men. "Bag him. Our client wants him alive. Make sure he doesn't try any of his magic tricks."

A rough sack suddenly blinded Reid, and a thick rope bound his hands. He squirmed against his bonds, but a heavy blow to the back of his head wiped the fight out of him.

He heard Fig's panicked voice calling his name before darkness claimed him.

20

Two reckless decisions altered Selene's life, but she only regretted one of them. Although she began to feel the stirrings of remorse for cursing Prince Leander, she couldn't help the gratitude for how it led her to Reid. She only lamented leaving him to save the children by himself. Deep down, she knew it was the right thing to do, yet pain nestled in her heart as she journeyed alone.

Every limb ached. She leaned against a long branch she fashioned into a walking stick for support as she limped along. If the map she had been following was correct, there were three days left of her journey on foot, and a day and a half by horse. There were no towns along the way, but she prayed she'd find a kind stranger on a horse, or who carted goods, to help her.

Dread pulsed through her veins. Doubt crept into the corners of her mind, and she swallowed thickly. She didn't account for how weak she'd feel three hours after she'd used wild magic. If she didn't pick up her pace soon, she'd likely arrive in four days instead of three.

Selene hoped and prayed that her plan would work. She wouldn't know how she could forgive herself if anything happened to the children... or Reid.

Trees bowed over her head, their branches stretching like menacing claws. Cicadas droned in the late summer afternoon, and the sun began to dip in the sky. The longer she moved, the more energy trickled back into her body. Relief flooded her like a wash of cool water on scorched skin, and she discarded the walking stick to pick up her pace.

As she sped along the road, she couldn't help but wonder which steward had betrayed the Arcane Order. Her thoughts flew to Kallisar and his pompous smile. It had been his idea to apprehend the Pied Piper to redeem herself. It would be convenient for him if his rival were to suddenly meet her end by the bounty hunters he sent after her. She didn't doubt he'd use any means to gain power—he didn't deserve his seat as a High Steward.

Selene shook her head. That was her jealousy talking, and worst of all, her father's voice echoing in her mind, haunting her for not securing a seat as High Steward. She couldn't blame Kallisar without solid evidence. It could be anyone in the Arcane Order—including Lysandriel, the Supreme High Steward.

Her insides wrung like a wet towel at the thought. No, it couldn't be Lysandriel. She was too good to betray the Order. Perhaps it was Ismara, the gentle High Steward hiding a malicious spirit behind her kind smile, or Vesperian, the man Selene swore had a vendetta against her. He'd always been the strictest among the leaders and graded her the harshest. Thalandros was also a possibility, but his opinion swayed like a boat lost at sea, tugged in whichever direction the strongest opinion was. He had no backbone to be seen.

However, in all likelihood, it could be any of the hundreds of stewards serving the Arcane Order. One wolf hid in sheep's clothing, and she had to discover their identity before it was too late.

Around the bend, a cloaked figure stood in the middle of the path. Selene came to a halt, her eyes narrowing on the person whose features were shadowed under their hood. Their height and build suggested a male, but they neither moved nor spoke a word. Something pricked at the back of her neck, and the hair on her arms raised.

Could it be another bounty hunter?

Selene reached into the well of her chaotic magic, knowing it might not play in her favor. Wild magic would surely make her incapacitated again, so unstable magic was better than nothing. Her fingers twitched, waiting to see what the figure would do.

The male stepped forward, removing his hood. From beneath his cloak, he revealed a black wand with a glowing, green crystal embedded in a silver moon design. Dark hair, glinting a midnight blue under the light, swept back in a medium-length, textured, cropped style. Deep, emerald eyes regarded her with mild curiosity. Selene tensed.

"High Steward Thalandros?" she asked slowly, hardly believing her eyes. Her hand shot to her chest, her fingers splayed as she gave a short bow of respect. "What are you doing here?"

"I've been tasked to oversee your progress. Lysandriel sent me to check on your status," he said, his voice quiet against the wind. His shoulders were hunched, and his steps timid.

Selene's brows furrowed. "Why now?"

"Because your time is nearly up. You have three days. She is worried you will not make it in time." He frowned, looking past her as if in search of someone. "Perhaps she is right. I do not see your prisoner with you."

"I know what this looks like," she started, taking a step closer. "But everyone is mistaken. The Pied Piper is not the villain we thought he was. There's something more sinister and bigger than we could have imagined. The children are in danger! I must speak with Lysandriel immediately so we can take action."

Concern flashed in his expression. "What danger do you speak of? You may tell me so I can relay the message to her."

Selene sighed in relief. Her prayers were being answered. "The children are being used to mine feralite! They weren't abducted but saved! I confirmed this with the bounty hunters and Rei—I mean, the Pied Piper. These *people* have found a trail leading to where the Piper is keeping them safe. We don't have much time! We must act now—"

"Slow down, Selene, it's alright," Thalandros said gently.

Her breath heaved, her heart pounding painfully. "It's not alright, High Steward. One of our own has betrayed the Order. A steward is heading the operation as we speak. Can't you see? Everything we thought about Reid is wrong, and we must help him save the children before it's too late!"

Thalandros took another step, and then another. Soon, he was close enough to reach out and pat her arm like a child. She shivered at his touch.

"Do you honestly believe him? This Pied Piper?" he asked.

"Yes. I know he can be trusted. He was one of the children who had been captured, but he managed to escape years ago."

"I see." Thalandros' usual mild-manneredness disappeared under a rigid posture. "This is much more serious than I thought."

"Yes," she agreed. "So, will you take me to Lysandriel? She must know of this treachery as soon as possible."

The thin fingers around her arm tightened just enough for her to notice. Pity marred his frown.

"I appreciate your honesty, Selene. You've put a lot of trust in me, for which I'm grateful. But... Lysandriel will never know of this."

Her breath stilled. "What?" Suddenly, he was too close for comfort as his deep green eyes bored into her. Once she thought him to be the weakest of the five High Stewards, but something in his aura shifted.

"You see, it would be unwise to allow this information to get out. Not when we're so close to perfection. The world needs this more than it needs you, especially when you're a danger to society."

Selene's pulse surged. Her tongue refused to work, and the ground tilted beneath her.

"You're..."

"What? Speak up so I may hear you."

His voice was too calm, too calculating.

Selene's gut twisted, and she carefully summoned her chaotic magic to the surface. "You're the steward who's taken the children," she hissed.

"Ah, ah," he tsked softly, his grasp tightening. Ice flooded her veins as his magic slithered like a snake around her core. "Let's not be too reckless. You've already proven you're not of sound mind. Cursing princes, letting villains escape, and now threatening a High Steward? I believe that's one too many strikes against you."

Selene gritted her teeth. "You don't deserve the title of High Steward. Lysandriel would never stand for your crimes."

"You're right. She wouldn't. She's too blind to see the possibilities of the future I have in store for Averayne, let alone all of Lioren. The children of the Divine deserve to be equal in all things, including magic. Feralite will be the answer for a better world."

Selene's eyes widened. "Feralite will destroy them. It's too unstable to wield."

"Oh, you of little faith," he said softly. "It is only a matter of time until I can refine it into a reliable source. I've spent over two decades perfecting the material, and I will not let you of all people ruin all that progress."

"At the expense of innocent children?"

"Yes. Their sacrifices are invaluable, and a mere moment of suffering for the good of Lioren. Think of the world as it could be, Selene, where no one will need to suffer again with the convenience of magic at their fingertips. There will be no divide between social classes. Stewards will no longer reign as supreme, but those more qualified, if given magic, can stand as the leaders we need. Isn't it unfair that some are born with magic and others are not? I can bridge that divide. I can be the change we desperately need."

For a moment, Selene hesitated. The tired, filthy faces of the children she gave oranges to in the alley appeared in her mind. It wasn't fair that they were left to fend for themselves on the streets, hungry and alone. If everyone had access to magic, more people could grow plentiful crops or help those in need. For those already gifted with magic, there wouldn't be a need for years of strenuous training to become a steward if the convenience of a stone could summon magic.

Perhaps the world would be a better place...

Yet, the memory of Reid's sullen face and the deep haunting sorrow in his eyes when he recounted his tale of being taken. How many children had suffered, and how many more would endure the exploitation thrust upon them?

Despite the chilling sensation of his magic hovering around Selene like a predator about to strike, she narrowed her eyes. "You can never reap good when the soil you've sown has trampled over the innocent. How many more years will you need to refine a crystal that does not wish to be tamed? It is not meant for human hands. The Divine would never want this. People don't need magic to be equal! They are valuable as human beings the way they are."

Her breath stuttered. The revelation of her words cut deeper than she anticipated. Her magic had defined every part of her life—it was the only source of her worth. But...

Perhaps Reid was right. She was worth more than the skills she could prove to her father. Every soul, with or without magic, had value, including Prince Leander.

The blood rushed from her face. In the face of Thalandros' wretched schemes, the weight of the curse she had placed on the prince crashed down on her.

Thalandros' magic sharpened like a knife in her chest. She couldn't breathe as he studied her with a passive expression. "How hypocritical. I thought perhaps you, of all people, could see the potential I hold for the world. After all, you've stooped low enough to curse a prince out of sheer *spite*. Your deed did not bring good, it only caused more pain. At least the pain I inflict is temporary in the name of peace to the world."

"Is it true peace?" she choked out. "Or merely a ploy for more power?"

His lips thinned as he tilted his head. "I tire of this conversation." With one step, he retreated along with his magic.

Selene coughed violently before sucking in the air she'd been denied. She glowered at him. "Why tell me all this?"

"Because you won't be alive for much longer. I thought perhaps you could have been reasonable enough to join my quest for peace, but I see you are of no use to me."

Thalandros tucked his wand within his robe and brandished a knife. The silver glinted against the setting sun, causing Selene's breath to hitch.

"Why not kill me with magic?" she asked, already knowing the answer. Death by magic would be recognizable and easily traced back to the one who cast the spell. She hoped the question would stall him.

He gave her a blank stare before sighing. "Weapons stir fewer questions. Now, if you hold still, this will be over quickly. I'll try to make it as painless as I can."

"Please, wait—"

Thalandros lunged for her. Selene fell back, but not before the metal sliced across her shoulder. A scream tore from her throat, but she called to the limited, chaotic magic within. He loomed over her, his dagger plunging toward her chest. Brilliant, rainbow light burst from her fingertips. Thousands of reflective, sparkling particles exploded like a powerful gust of wind.

Thalandros grunted, shielding his eyes as he flew backward. Dust and glitter spewed into the air as he fell. Selene scrambled to her feet, desperate to run, but a force held her back. The blade ripped into the hem of her dress, pinning her to the ground. Thalandros leapt onto her, eyes blazing as he pulled another knife from his cloak.

Selene felt the ground for anything that would help her. Grabbing a fistful of dirt, she threw it in his eyes. Thalandros sputtered as she bucked him off her. Rolling, her skirt ripped free from the knife, and she reached for a rock. A low growl sounded before strong arms wrapped around her waist, throwing her to the ground. The knife stabbed downward, but she moved, and it sliced her cheek instead. With a scream, she cracked the rock against his temple.

Time slowed, but his eyes fluttered shut. Blood trickled from his head. Her heart raced when his weight collapsed on her. Panic wormed in her throat as she shoved him off her and scrambled away. She didn't check to see if his pulse still beat, or if breath rose from his chest. Selene ran as fast as her legs could carry her.

Had she killed him?

The implications sank its teeth into her coiling gut. She had no witnesses, no prisoner, and only her word against a dead High Steward. If he lived, she knew he would kill her before she could step foot into the Arcane Sanctum, or use his position of power to persuade the others of her guilt. The mark on his forehead would be proof of her crime. There was no other choice but to run.

The distance she put between herself and Reid felt like the most significant danger of all. If Thalandros had found her, it was possible his men had found Reid, too. Her throat burned, muscles quivered, but she would not stop until she found him. She prayed she wasn't too late.

21

Everything in Reid's body ached when he woke. Water dripped from the ceiling, pooling in a greenish puddle in the corner of the dark cell. The air tasted stale and musty, and a sliver of moonlight flickered over the thick, iron chains around his wrists and ankles. The metal clanked as he sat up, but a stabbing sensation bored through his skull with the movement.

He didn't know how long he'd lain on the cold, damp stone floor, but he didn't have to guess where he'd been taken. A shiver ran down his spine. The chilling, yet familiar hold of the chains could only mean one thing.

He'd been captured.

His core went cold. There was nothing there—no magic, no spark of threads to the wild he'd known all his life. The chains had been magically enchanted to seal his magic. But what else had they taken?

He placed a hand over his chest, and his breath stilled when he couldn't feel the soft lump that usually perched there.

"Petunia?" he whispered.

Drip. Drip. Drip.

The steady beat of water answered his call. Ice sank to his stomach. Had she been hurt when they transported him here? Did they take her away? All the possibilities churned his gut, making him want to heave.

"Petunia... are you there, girl?"

Nothing. Dread gripped him by the throat. His eyes stung with the threat of tears, but he choked them back.

Something scurried to his right. His head shot up toward the tiny, rectangular window, and a small silhouette shadowed his face. Relief bloomed with his smile.

"Petunia!"

The cloaked rat scampered down a supporting beam, racing toward him. Reid opened his hands out and scooped her up with a breathless chuckle. He planted kisses on her head, and Petunia's nose twitched, her whiskers shivering.

"I knew you were made of tougher stuff," he said. "For a moment, I thought I lost you. Who else would put up with my whining?"

Petunia leaned in, pressing her nose against his jaw.

"I know, I know," he sighed. "Not the time for jokes, but what else will brighten the place up? Gotta make light of the situation."

She stared at him.

"That was a little funny, admit it."

Petunia blinked slowly.

"Fine, it's not my best, but I think you can forgive me considering the circumstances."

Her nose twitched again, and then she turned to gesture to the window.

"Right, we need to make a plan. Do you think you could locate some keys or a pick?"

Petunia nodded. Heavy footsteps echoed down the hall, and her ears flattened back.

"I'll be alright," he reassured her with a small smile. "Now, hurry and help get me out of here."

Petunia leaped from his hands and scampered up the wooden post and through the bars of the small window. The door creaked open, and the so-called mayor entered the cell with a haughty smirk.

"About time you woke up. Didn't know if we killed you back there, but I'm glad you're still breathing," the mayor said.

The chains rattled as Reid placed a hand to his heart mockingly. "Aw, Burke. I'm touched. Didn't realize you cared for me so much."

Burke sneered. "I wouldn't get too cocky, Piper. Doesn't mean we won't be killing you soon."

"Y'know," Reid said, leaning back against the wall. "There have been a few people who've said that, yet surprisingly, I'm *still* here."

"Not by morning, you won't. The boss steward wants a public execution, and the gallows have your name written all over it."

"Gallows? Couldn't you have been a little more creative?"

Burke glared. "If I had it my way, you'd be receiving much worse. You've caused us enough problems, Piper. Now we're going to have to relocate to a different feralite source 'cause of you."

Reid's muscles stiffened, and his smile wilted. "Relocate the children? Where?"

"You're not privy to that information," Burke sneered, folding his arms.

"C'mon, I'm a dead man anyway, right? What's it to you if I know or not?"

Burke regarded him silently before a slow, chilling smile crept on his lips. He took a step, then another, until he crouched down to Reid's eye level.

"I suppose you make a good point," Burke said, his grin widening. "Rumor has it there's a feralite source down south, deep in the desert dunes—far from any civilization... or wood sprites."

Reid's stomach twisted. He forced himself to keep calm, but dread coated his insides.

"Heard those creatures aren't so fond of fire," Burke continued. "Had to see it for myself. The monastery went up in flames faster than I expected."

"You're bluffing."

"Am I?"

Reid's molars clenched. "There's a special place in the void for you. I don't think you know what you've done."

"It's no longer our problem." Burke stood, looming over him smugly. "You, however, are still a problem that will be dealt with in the morning. Try and catch some sleep. It'll be your last."

The mayor strode away, shut the cell door, and locked it behind him. Somewhere in the forest, Fig could be injured, or she could have escaped the flames. The possibilities were endless, and each one made him more nauseous to think of. The only thing he could take solace in was that the forest and the Divine would remember their crimes. But Reid feared the wood sprites wouldn't be able to retaliate in time. They were too far away, bound to the forest with no way to seek justice on their own.

If Reid had anything to say about it, he would gladly serve it for them. If he lived past tomorrow, he swore he'd make things right in the world.

He glanced at his chains, wondering if Petunia would find what he needed to free himself from the dam around his magic. His mind raced, thinking of different plans of escape.

This wasn't how this was going to end. Reid would go down fighting if it meant he could free the children and see Selene one last time.

22

Selene added another crime to her list as she spurred a farmer's horse into a gallop. One day, she would repay whoever owned the animal and bring it back if—by the Divine's will—she somehow made it out alive.

The wind blew through her hair, and her eyes hardened with resolve. She never should have left Reid to go alone. It made sense why he was reluctant to go to the Arcane Sanctum. He was right. One of the High Stewards of all people had betrayed them. And Thalandros would have sent Reid straight to prison and left him to rot, or worse, sentenced him to death.

Her teeth clenched at the injustice of it all. Thalandros had sent the bounty hunters to kill her. He wanted her out of the way and perhaps to blame Reid for her death. But as long as she lived, she wouldn't stand by while Thalandros exploited helpless children for the opportunity to gift magic to everyone. It wasn't selfless, it was selfish. As much as Thalandros claimed it was to help improve the world, there was nothing but greed and pride behind his self-righteous monologues. He'd only make a profit distributing feralite to everyone.

Selene urged the horse north into the Glimmerwood forest. Reid had said the old monastery was deep in the woods by the river bend, and she followed the sound of the rushing waters nearby. Dirt and river rocks spewed beneath the horse's hooves as she raced alongside the river upstream.

A thick, ashy scent filled Selene's nose. Her eyes watered when fumes thickened the air, and her heart plummeted to her stomach as a plume of gray smoke billowed above the treetops.

"Reid!"

The horse slowed his gait, his ears flattening. A nervous snort escaped him when she directed him into the copse of trees. Nonetheless, Selene kicked against his flanks, urging him into a gallop. The trees blurred around her, and a chilling sensation wrapped around her insides. Smoke slithered between the trees, suffocating the air in her chest. The sun set behind the mountains, blanketing her in darkness. The last conversation she had with Reid echoed in her mind.

"Reid, don't—promise me you'll be safe. Please."
"No promises."

They burst into a clearing, and she gasped. The monastery was little more than a skeleton of charred wooden beams and blackened stone. Selene slid off the horse before the animal came to a stop, and she stumbled into the ash. Orange flames crept toward the trees, consuming everything in their path.

"Reid! Where are you?" she shouted.

Selene staggered back when a wave of water crashed onto the fire. The flames hissed, and clouds of white steam rose into the air, mingling with the suffocating smoke.

"That's it, keep it coming!" a light, feminine voice cried out.

Another surge of river water poured onto the fire, and Selene's eyes widened. River sprites rose from the bend, their hands caressing the water's surface, then a column of water shot toward the sky and crashed into the remaining writhing flames. Their translucent, humanoid bodies were made of crystal-clear water, and their clothing consisted of various river plants. On land, moonlight illuminated a feminine figure made of bark, vines, and moss standing amidst the chaos.

A wood sprite.

Selene had never seen a sprite of any kind before. Most people never did, since the creatures stayed reclusive and distant from humans. Was this the sprite Reid had spoken of?

The wood sprite turned, her bright green eyes pinning Selene to the spot. The creature scowled, and before she could blink, vines whipped toward her, wrapping around her waist. Suddenly, there was no ground beneath her feet as the vines lifted her into the air.

"Hasn't your kind done enough?" the wood sprite hissed.

"Wait—wait!" Selene choked out. The vines tightened, making it difficult to breathe. "Reid! He sent me. Where is he? Are the children safe?"

Something in the wood sprite's eyes shifted. Slowly, Selene's boots touched solid ground once more, and the vines retreated.

"What is your name?"

"Selene," she said, clutching her aching abdomen.

"You know Reid?" the wood sprite asked warily.

"Yes. I'm here to help him and the children. Where are they?"

The river sprites looked at each other, a frown on their watery faces. The wood sprite took a step forward, mirroring their sullen expressions.

"Taken. They've all been taken."

Numbness crept through Selene's limbs. Her knees quivered, threatening to collapse, but she raised an arm to lean against a tree for support. Bile crept up the back of her throat, and she blinked rapidly, attempting to unhear the words turning her world into a living nightmare.

"Is he...?"

"He's still alive," the wood sprite supplied gently. "They took him a few hours ago. I assume they're taking them back to Hamlin, where Reid had rescued the children."

Her mind stuttered with the information, but she inhaled a deep breath filled with lingering smoke.

"I have to save them... I—I should leave now and—"

"You won't make it in time on horseback," the wood sprite said. "I doubt they will keep him alive for very long."

Tears pricked at the back of her eyes. Would she be too late to save him?

"Then... what should I do? I can't let him die. I have to do something!"

The wood sprite approached until she was a mere step away. A bark-like finger raised toward Selene's face, but she didn't flinch. The sprite wiped something away before bringing the tear before her.

A slow smile spread on the sprite's face. "And you won't do it alone. It's about time someone else should care for him. I won't abandon him either. Besides... mankind has abused these innocent children and the destructive powers of feralite for far too long."

More tears slipped down Selene's face as relief washed over her. "Will you come with me then?"

"That I cannot do. I am bound to the forest the same way the river sprites are bound to the river. But I can call on someone who can."

The wood sprite turned and began to hum. The sound reminded Selene of how the wind whistled through the branches, how autumn leaves danced on the breeze, and how the forest seemed to sing within the silence. Peace washed over her, quieting the anxious thoughts raging through her mind. In moments, something rippled against the night sky—something enormous. Selene's eyes snapped up to the stars, catching a dark shape concealing the moon before it glided in their direction.

The once camouflaged shape revealed itself as it descended. Energy crackled in its wake, and a hum vibrated through Selene's body. Its luminous green wings, etched with silvery tips, unfurled like giant sails upon the breeze. Two long tails trailed behind its body, catching the wind like rippling satin. Its long, fuzzy body gleamed like a shimmering pearl against the stars, and it landed gently in the scorched clearing. Selene gaped, taking in the translucent veins, four golden circles embedded in its wings, and the velvety, yellow antenna.

A Lunathera.

The giant moths had only been sighted a handful of times throughout history. Long ago, when Glimmerwood was very young, the Lunathera were woven with starlight and twilight dust by the Divine to protect the forests and their inhabitants. They answered to the forest alone, giving aid when called. Selene never dreamed one would appear to her in her lifetime.

"Her name is Nyra," the wood sprite said, breaking Selene's rapt attention on the mystical creature. "She will help you travel to Hamlin."

Nyra stepped forward, her large eyes never blinking, but Selene sensed a deep kindness within those black orbs. She stood, frozen in awe at the giant creature before her. The power humming around Nyra overwhelmed her. Selene had never felt such magnificence in energy in all her years around the most powerful stewards. She approached hesitantly, curtseying low before the Lunathera.

"I am honored, Lady Nyra."

Nyra bowed her head in acknowledgement.

"Nyra, make haste to Hamlin," the wood sprite said. "It is time the humans learned to leave nature alone. Go, quickly now before it's too late!"

"But—the stewards!" Selene's eyes widened in remembrance. "I need help from Lady Lysandriel. Perhaps if you send a message, they will listen."

The wood sprite nodded in understanding. "I will send a messenger bird for you. The children will need as much aid as possible."

"Tell her to meet me in Hamlin. The children are in danger, and Thalandros is the perpetrator."

"Very well."

Nyra knelt on her front legs, making it easy for Selene to climb onto her soft body. Since there was no saddle to sit on, she clung to the silky hair instead. With a flap of her wings, Nyra took off into the sky. Selene's heartbeat accelerated as she watched the ground grow more distant.

Suddenly, a realization dawned on her. "Wait, what is your name?" Selene called out to the wood sprite.

"It's Fig!"

"Thank you, Fig. I am indebted to you."

"Consider the debt paid when you rescue Reid and the children. Put an end to those who dared burn Glimmerwood!"

Selene nodded, her stomach flipping when Nrya surged forward. The wind chilled her skin, her teeth chattering, but her heart filled with hope.

"I'm coming for you, Reid. Just wait for me a little longer."

23

R eid stared at the ceiling, unable to sleep—not when his death was scheduled for the morning. His only reliable means of escape hadn't returned, and he wondered if anything had happened to Petunia. If she didn't return in time, he would certainly meet the Divine sooner rather than later.

Reid needed a backup plan.

There were no others occupying the cells to rally to his side. He'd have to do this alone. The chains were bolted to the wall and floor, and there was nothing in the room to damage them. Reid groped the walls, hoping to find some loose stone or a weak latch in the bolts. When that failed, he bent on hands and knees to probe the dirt floor for any give, and scratched at the surface, but the ground was too dry and compacted. Even if he managed to succeed, it would take hours to dig his way out, and he'd still have his chains to worry about.

There was only one other idea he could try if he were desperate. A shudder ran down his spine, but if it came down to it, he'd dislocate his fingers to wriggle out of the chains if need be.

He hoped it wouldn't come to that. Reid rather liked his fingers and would prefer his bones to be intact.

Flopping to the ground, he sighed. "C'mon girl, where are you?"

The air shifted. An unsettling hush fell over his already quiet cell, and his skin prickled with goosebumps. The chains were supposed to suppress his magic, but an energy buzzed through his veins. It wasn't his magic—something older, perhaps *ancient*, electrified the air.

Reid stood, his eyes transfixed on the small window above his head. A ripple moved through the sky as if it were made of glassy water. Torches sputtered out, and confused shouting echoed in the distance. Two men rushed past his cell, their eyes wide with fear. A clamoring of voices rose in the air.

"Can you feel it?"

"What is that?"

"The feralite! It's reacting to something!"

"What's going on?"

"Don't touch it!"

Another familiar energy pulsed behind the cell walls, crackling like lightning. He knew that chaotic force—the way it sputtered and hissed beneath his hands as a child—he knew it well. Reid's eyes widened as he backed away as far as he could.

An unnatural pitch rang in the air like a snapped string on a lute, followed by a roaring bang. Reid crouched, covering his head as the ground shook beneath him. A wave of heat stormed against the walls, rattling the bars of his cell. Dust rained down on him, filling his lungs.

More panicked shouts resounded outside. Reid's heart drummed painfully against his ribs as he gradually stood. It's a miracle that only part of the feralite erupted; if all of it had, the entire town would have been engulfed in flames.

It wasn't uncommon for feralite to react destructively, but it was the first he'd felt it respond to an ancient energy. He wasn't sure if it was wild magic or another source entirely, but hope welled inside him. Perhaps Fig survived the fires, and the forest had come for vengeance.

The sound of claws scratching against wood sounded by the window. A small critter chirped before scurrying toward him.

"Petunia?"

Some of her fur had been singed, smoke whisping from her golden coat, but metal gleamed between her teeth. She jumped onto his shoulder, panting and dropping the small, cool pick into the palm of his hand.

"Oh, good girl," he breathed a sigh of relief while holding her close. Petunia nodded, flopping into his lap as he began to work on his chains.

Dawn was approaching, and he needed to work fast.

Selene's stomach dropped, plummeting past the clouds of smoke and into the explosions. From her vantage point on Nyra, people hurried through the streets of Hamlin like frightened ants trying to maintain order amid the chaos. Flames tore through timbered walls, turning the rooftops black. Men lined up to extinguish the fires consuming the town.

Selene's breath caught.

"Reid—no!"

A low hum vibrated from Nyra's soft body beneath her. It pulsed a lulling melody, quieting the fears rampaging through her heart. The air shimmered like a million flecks of starlight, wrapping around her like an embrace.

"Do not fear."

Selene jolted at the foreign voice in her mind. The gentle, feminine tone made her pause.

"Reid is safe. The feralite reacts to the ancient powers I hold, but all will be well. Use this opportunity to slip unnoticed through the shadows."

Selene exhaled a long breath. "Thank you, Lady Nyra."

The moth sailed through the sky, circling the city and the screaming men below. No one looked up, and if they had, Nyra blended with the backdrop of stars. Gently, Nyra descended, landing in an open field near the city.

"The forest remembers. I have taken an oath to not commit violence against mankind, but I will linger long enough for the feralite to continue reacting. It is all I can do. I entrust you to stop the corrupted before they continue to lay waste to the Divine's creations."

"I promise I will do everything in my power to stop them," Selene vowed.

"I sense Reid is held in a prison north of the town square, left of the mayor's abode. Good luck, and may the Divine be with you."

Nyra knelt, allowing Selene to slide gently off her back. The world spun for a dizzying moment before she steadied herself on the grass.

"Thank you," Selene said. A gust of wind surged as Nyra ascended into the sky, leaving behind sparkling dust in her wake.

Selene wasted no time. She dashed toward the town illuminated by flames, slipping through the alleys and sticking to the shadows. Men and women rushed past with sloshing buckets of water to put out the fires, allowing her to race across the town square unnoticed. Her pulse thundered in her ears, and she feared it could be heard throughout the whole town.

Following Nyra's instructions, she slipped between homes until she found the prison adjacent to the mayor's office she'd visited months ago. Over a dozen people were rushing barrels in wagons away, while others poured water on the fire two houses down. No guards were stationed in front of the prison, perhaps too occupied with helping put out the flames, and Selene crept inside. The halls were narrow, dark, and dank. The smell of filth and stale water permeated the air as she stole through the corridors.

The cells were empty—no children, prisoners, or Reid in sight. Panic ate through her core until she spotted a stone staircase. Following the path, she bounded down the spiral steps. Two sconces wavered with flickering flames about to burn out, bathing the hall in a dim and eerie light. The cells on both sides of her were empty, but movement caught her eye at the end of the passageway. Chains rattled, and clinking metal echoed in her ears.

Selene's feet moved faster than her thoughts. Her heart pounded a joyous song of relief, hope, and anticipation as she bounded toward the last cell.

"Reid!"

The shadowed figure behind the bars stood, and the chains clanked with the movement. Selene skidded to a stop before the cell, gasping at the bruises littering Reid's face. One eye was shut, swollen a dark purple, his lip split, but he managed a half-delirious smile. His one good eye, ringed with exhaustion, widened.

"Violet?"

The sound of her name, hoarse from his throat, carved a hole in her chest. Petunia perked beside Reid, her teeth grating in excitement. Selene fumbled with the door, forgetting it would be locked. With a frustrated growl, she blasted chaotic magic into it, and the handle melted into a steaming pile of green goop. Selene threw the creaking door open.

She took only one step inside before he crossed the distance within two long strides.

"Reid—!"

Selene couldn't get the following words out. His shackled, trembling hands wrapped around her waist, pulling her in.

Then his mouth was on hers.

It wasn't soft or hesitant, but filled with a ragged desperation and longing. In one feverish breath, she sensed every unspoken tension, every touch he'd held back, and every word he never got to profess.

Her thoughts scattered like a whirl of dandelion seeds lost against a torrential wind. But then she lost herself to the fervency of his kiss. Her fingers curled into his torn shirt, clinging to him to steady her buckling knees.

Reid pulled away too soon. His forehead leaned against hers, breathless, with his eyes searching hers.

"I've been waiting to do that since Brambelune. I've been kicking myself ever since I left without kissing you," he murmured.

Her swollen lips parted, yearning for more.

He chuckled softly. "I hope it wasn't against the rules."

Selene swallowed, taking in every discolored bruise on his face to the crooked grin on his lips. "I'll make an exception for you," she whispered. Something squeaked, and she glanced down. Petunia folded her arms, and Selene swore she saw a smirk on her lips as if to say, *It's about time.*

"Good." He leaned closer, his thumb caressing her cheek. "Because even if it was, I was planning on breaking it again and again."

His breath caressed her jaw, and a shiver raced down her spine. Her eyes flicked to his mouth.

"Please do."

24

This must be a dream, Reid thought as he brushed a shaky thumb over Selene's cheek. Perhaps the explosions had knocked him unconscious, and the Divine granted him one last glimpse of the woman he loved.

Yet, the scent of her lavender hair filled his head, her flushed skin warmed his chilled fingers, and their kiss still hummed through his body. Reid didn't know what he had done to deserve this moment, but if this were an act of divine mercy, he'd take it.

"How did you find me?" he whispered.

"I had some help."

"Help?" he asked, tilting his head. He glanced at Petunia, but the rat shrugged her shoulders.

"From Fig," Selene said, and Reid blinked, unable to process her words. Then, Selene supplied an explanation, diving into her story about meeting Thalandros on the road, escaping into the woods, meeting Fig, and fleeing to Hamlin on a Lunathera.

The stale, musty prison air caught in his throat.

"A Lunathera?" he murmured. No one had glimpsed the ancient creatures for over two centuries. But the forest had been provoked. His thoughts spun, and answers clicked into place. "No wonder the feralite was reacting."

"She's still out there, giving us the distraction we need," Selene said.

"Then we shan't waste this opportunity."

Reid leaned in, wanting to savor Selene's touch, perhaps for the last time, but the moment was broken by the mayor's voice barking orders at the men. There was no time.

Selene's eyes fluttered shut, but he sighed. "I wish I could oblige, Violet," he said, reluctantly pulling away. "We have to save the children first."

Disappointment flickered in her gaze before hardening with resolve. "Let me help you with those chains."

Reid eyed the steaming green puddle Selene had made of the door. "Wait, before you do that—"

He blinked, and the chains on his hands and feet transformed into a flower link instead of cold iron. Chuckling, he dusted the flowers off himself.

"You could have turned me into a pile of goop if you weren't careful," he teased.

"And risk never being able to kiss you again? Never." She smiled coyly before adding, "I think I'm understanding how to direct my limited magic better."

"Lucky me."

Petunia bounded over to the flowers, nosing through them, but the message in her glance was unmistakable.

I'm happy for you, but you can't back out now.

His lips quirked ruefully. He certainly had made things complicated with that kiss. He crossed a line he couldn't undo, but if he didn't make it out alive after everything was said and done, he would die with the memory of her lips and a seed of hope that she loved him in return.

He reached over and slipped his hand into hers. "Now, let's go."

Reid tugged on her hand, motioned to Petunia, and ran through the empty corridor. Petunia caught up, leaping onto his pant leg with ease while he was in mid-motion before burrowing into his vest.

Reid glanced behind him, giving Selene's hand a firm squeeze. "No matter what happens next, don't come and try to save me, okay? Just focus on the children," he whispered.

Panic danced in her eyes. "I don't think I can do that," she said.

"You have to promise me you'll put the children first. They deserve a future—I don't deserve it as much as they do."

"Yes, you do," she said sternly as he paused at the stairwell. "You deserve more than you're willing to admit."

A seed of warmth sprouted in his chest, followed by the dark images of his past—of Tomas, who never made it.

"I think I can start believing that after I've saved them. But I appreciate hearing it all the same."

He kept his back to the wall, pausing before every corner they turned.

"Where do you think they're hiding them?" Selene asked.

"My first guess is somewhere close where Burke can keep an eye on them. He's the second in command to the steward."

They reached the entrance, and Reid flattened himself against the wall when he heard someone approaching, then signaled for Selene to keep moving after the footsteps faded. Reid felt the pull of his pipe, like a familiar melody whispering to him, and he followed that instinct toward the mayor's office. He opted for the back door, crouching low to avoid being seen.

A loud *bang* echoed behind the rattling windows. The ground shook, throwing him off balance, but he caught himself against the wall.

"The Piper!" someone shouted outside. "The prisoner is missing!"

"Ah, spells," Reid muttered. He thought they'd have a little more time before they noticed he was gone.

Quietly, he opened the door and was met with a small, quaint room, a crackling furnace, and the scent of stale candy. The cuckoo clocks on the walls ticked in the silence as he tiptoed over the rug. Petunia climbed down his pant leg, her whiskers twitching.

"Do you sense anything, girl?"

Petunia circled the rug, her nose hovering over the ground, before she stopped in the center. She furiously scratched the carpet, squeaking and chittering.

"Looks like she found something," Reid said, sighing in relief. He grabbed one corner of the rug, and Selene tugged on the other, and together, they rolled the rug away from the floor. A trap door with cold, iron bolts lay in the middle of the floor.

Reid knelt to the ground, picking at the daunting lock with the thin, round piece of metal Petunia had retrieved in the prison. Sweat dotted his brow the longer the time ticked on the cuckoo clocks. The minute hand in the shape of a squirrel seemed to mock him as he focused on the task.

Click!

Reid expelled a long breath. "Finally."

Dread sank like an icy stone into his stomach when he glanced up.

A pale hand wrapped around the back of Selene's throat. A menacing black wand with an emerald crystal lodged under her jaw. Surprise and fear glistened in her wide, cerulean eyes. Dark blue hair, almost black, swept across a scowling face. A deep, dark bruise and dried blood painted the man's temple. A deranged glint flashed in his eyes.

"Use your magic, and she dies," the man said in a deep, sinister tone. "Let's talk."

Reid's pulse roared in his ears, his blood growing cold as he slowly turned and raised his hands in a pacifying manner. He had never met the steward in charge of the feralite operation, but he had heard his voice as a child. There was no mistaking his identity.

This was the same steward from his childhood.

"Let her go. We can talk like civil men without threatening a lady," Reid said calmly despite the quiver running down his spine.

"Unfortunately, we are past civil pleasantries. You've jeopardized everything I have built, and I will ensure you do not do it again."

"Thalandros, wait—" Selene cried.

Rage burned in Reid's chest when Thalandros' fingers tightened over her neck. A sad squeak cut off whatever else she wished to say.

"Please," Reid said, his arms instinctively reaching toward her, "don't hurt her. Hurt me. I'm the one you want."

"I'm afraid she will become collateral damage either way. A pity. She had such potential to help me," Thalandros said.

"I beg of you," Reid whispered. "Do not harm her. Take me and leave her out of this."

A faint scuttle sounded behind Thalandros. Reid noticed the flash of golden fur, the barred teeth, and the determination in her beady, black eyes. Petunia bounded over the wood and lunged for the back of Thalandros' robe. Within a single breath, Petunia sank her teeth into the man's ear.

Thalandros howled and staggered backward. His hold on Selene loosened.

"Run!" Reid yelled.

Thalandros ripped Petunia away from him with a growl. Reid's chest constricted. His heart stilled.

Thalandros thrust his wand toward him, and Reid's body lifted into the air. The world whizzed in a blur of colors as an invisible force lifted him and hurled him backward. A roar exploded against him as he crashed into the window. Wood splintered. Glass shattered.

For a breathless moment, he was weightless—suspended in time until he collapsed onto the cobbled stone.

25

S hards of glass burst like an exploding star. They shimmered against the fires raging in the night. Selene couldn't hear herself screaming as she ran to Reid. Petunia was nowhere to be seen, and the man she loved had collapsed in a motionless heap. She held her breath—

Something slammed into her and she cried in pain. An invisible force crushed her against the wall, her breath flattened, and her throat tightened.

Footsteps crunched over glass, slowly approaching her.

Selene strained to glance at him. "Everything you aim to accomplish will only destroy the ones you seek to help!"

"There is no reasoning with you," Thalandros sighed. "There is more the world needs than pathetic *vermin*."

Good, she got him talking. Selene reached into her core, calling forth the chaos within.

"Reid is more of a man than you will ever be!"

Thalandros smirked, and his face drew closer. "Oh, you poor, misguided thing. The world will only remember him as the villain he truly is. And you? You will be nothing more than a selfish *enchantress*, rejected by the only man who meant anything to her."

Her teeth ground together. "You won't get away with this."

"That's the thing..." he said, whipping out a dagger—the very blade he had used to try and kill her the first time. "I already have."

The magic within her wouldn't come. Every part of her had been silenced by Thalandros' magic smashing her against the wall. Panic flitted through her veins. Selene screwed her eyes shut, waiting for him to strike. But the blow never came.

Glass cracked under footsteps. Selene hesitantly opened her eyes. Thalandros was walking away from her.

And toward Reid.

A few men from the village burst from the thick smoke and raced toward Thalandros. "There's the Piper!" one of the men cried.

"Wait! Stop—!" Selene screamed.

Thalandros raised a hand, and the men halted.

"Allow me."

"No! Get away from him! I'm right here, kill me instead!" she begged. "Don't hurt him!"

"Like I've said before," Thalandros murmured, "you will get your turn."

The blade glinted against the flames tearing through the village. Smoke clouded her chest and blurred her vision, and tears burned down her cheeks.

"No!"

Thalandros crouched next to Reid and lifted the dagger. Panic blared through every beat of her heart. The air stilled. The chaotic pool of magic calmed—something within her snapped. The threads of wild magic within the air, the ground, and every living thing around her roared to life. It flooded her veins and every fiber of her soul.

Magic sizzled through the smoky haze, flaring and thundering in rageful fits. The blazing fires quivered. Thalandros staggered back, collapsing onto the stone. The men trembled, reeling in shock as the ground cracked beneath them.

A blast of wind encircled them. Selene stepped from the wall, breaking the unseen force like a brittle chain. An inferno burned every inch of her skin, but the warmth did not sear her. Instead, it radiated like a thousand stars, pouring light from her core.

Slowly, her body lifted from the ground. She levitated, poised above the gaping High Steward. The winds howled, forming a tempest of crackling energy. Debris hurtled in all directions, striking Thalandros' men.

Thalandros raised his wand, deflecting the flying chairs, cuckoo clocks, and shards of glass. In the center, Reid remained untouched.

Thalandros diverged some splinters of wood in her direction, but they fell before they could pierce her.

"You can't keep that up for long," Thalandros hissed. "You will meet your end using that much wild magic."

Selene glanced at Reid, who remained limp and unmoving, and her heart cracked into a dark chasm. Then, she pierced a glare toward Thalandros.

"So be it. I will burn out like the stars to save him."

Selene raised her hand out, and Thalandros clawed at his neck. From the flurry of wind, chains whipped out and restrained him. His black wand clattered to the ground. With her other hand, the wand floated into the air before snapping like a twig. His head reared back as he yelled in agony—a black brand in the image of a cracked, five-pointed star etched into his neck.

"No!" Thalandros roared.

"You will never hurt anyone again," she whispered.

The fires within her dimmed. Her muscles quivered, and the twisting flurry died into a faint breeze. As soon as her boots touched the ground, her knees crashed into the cobblestone. Thalandros squirmed in his chains, cursing against the wind.

"Selene..." a hoarse voice called out.

Her eyes snapped to Reid, who clutched his arm. Several tears cut through his white sleeves, revealing trickling blood beneath. A grin bloomed on her lips.

"Reid," she breathed like a sigh of relief.

He crawled closer, grunting in pain as he reached for her hand. "What did you do?"

"I did what I had to do to protect you."

The confusion in his eyes melted into horror. "Oh, Selene... no. You foolish, foolish woman!"

Every muscle quivered beneath her skin, rippling with exhaustion. She graced him with a small smile as her eyes began to droop.

"I see you've taken care of things."

Selene's head whipped around. High Steward Ismara strode toward them, her purple staff glowing with pow-er. Behind her, a band of stewards marched, their presence imposing and their steps purposeful. Fig's message had gotten through—they had come to help.

Thalandros turned, his face etched with surprise, before he masked it with panic. "Ismara, I'm so relieved! Selene has gone mad! Apprehend her at once. Look at what she's done to me!"

Lady Ismara marched up to him, pointing her staff directly at his chest. "I think it's you we need to apprehend," she said coldly.

Thalandros gaped. "L-lady Ismara—"

"We received a message that you threatened one of our stewards and are in charge of a ring of child labor," Ismara shot back, her voice unwavering.

Thalandros scoffed. "Would you believe the word of a jealous outcast and a criminal over your fellow High Steward?"

Ismara's deep brown eyes narrowed. "No, I would believe it from the wood sprites who protect the forests. Do you think your title excuses you from justice? We are not above the laws we uphold."

Selene exhaled a sigh of relief. The forest had come to her aid in more ways than one, and she prayed in gratitude for their help.

Thalandros swallowed, his voice hitching. "You're being manipulated, Ismara. Don't fall prey to their lies!"

Ismara didn't back down, tightening her grip on her staff. "Then you won't mind if we investigate," she stated firmly. "If there's truly nothing to hide, you have nothing to fear."

"He's the perpetrator!" Selene cried out, using what little energy lingered in her body. "He's been exploiting the children and using the feralite crystals to create unstable magic artifacts."

"They're stored in the crates," Reid said weakly.

Ismara eyed him warily. Selene didn't know if they would trust Reid, but after a moment, the High Steward raised her hand in a signal.

One of the stewards hurried over to examine the crates filled with glowing crystals. He grimaced, holding his hand cautiously above them. "These are saturated with raw, wild magic. It's dangerous to even be near them."

Lady Ismara turned to Selene. "Is this true?"

Selene nodded. "The children are the only ones who can safely mine it because of their untapped magic. He plans to use the feralite to bring magic to all non-magical people."

Ismara frowned deeply. "This cannot go unpunished."

"You have no idea what you're doing!" Thalandros snarled. "I was trying to revolutionize the world!"

"At the cost of innocent lives?" Ismara shot back. "We are meant to protect people, not exploit them."

Darkness tempted Selene's vision. Every muscle screamed in protest until she could no longer hold herself up. She collapsed onto the ground, her energy flickering out like dying embers. Reid tightened his grip on her hand.

"Are you all right?" he asked. He struggled to sit up, but a steward rushed to her side and propped her up. She could barely keep her head upright.

A scuffle sounded behind her. From her peripheral, the children began climbing out of the hatch with Petunia at the lead. They gathered around Ismara, clinging to one another. One of the older boys, trembling, stepped forward. "Are you here to save us?"

Ismara kneeled to his level. "Yes, we're here to save you. Who did this to you?"

The little boy pointed to Thalandros. "He made us work day and night. He said if we didn't, he'd hurt us."

Lady Ismara stood and looked down at Thalandros with pure contempt. "You will answer for this."

"They don't know what they're saying—" Thalandros protested until she waved her purple staff. Magic bound his lips together.

"I've heard enough." Lady Ismara turned to Selene. "Good work. You did well bringing this to our attention."

Selene hesitated, her eyes threatening to close, but she glanced at Reid. "What about Reid? The Pied Piper?"

Ismara's eyes moved to Reid, assessing him. "We will need to investigate further."

Selene's heart dropped. "No! He's not a villain—he saved the children! He risked his life for them!"

"Don't hurt him!" a little girl cried out, standing before him. More children protested.

"He saved us from the bad people!"

"Don't take him away!"

"He's our hero!"

Ismara studied the children, then cast her gaze to the growing crowd of soot-covered men and women. The stewards brandished their wands threateningly, but the crowd raised their hands in surrender. At last, she turned her attention on Reid.

"Then he deserves a hero's reward," Ismara said gently.

Selene's lashes fluttered closed, a faint smile on her lips.

"Selene?" Reid asked as his hands cradled her face.

Relief washed through her like a cooling balm before the darkness swallowed her. Somewhere in the distance, Nyra hummed a triumphant song over the smoky dawn.

26

Reid rubbed slow circles over the back of Selene's hand, willing her to wake. Gauzy, blue curtains fluttered in the crisp autumn wind, allowing the scent of fallen leaves and the hint of musky sandalwood to fill the infirmary. Several colorful, bubbling potions lined her bedstand, and he wondered if any of them were helping Selene.

Her alabaster skin took on a paler sheen, and her fingers chilled his hand. Warm, white blankets enveloped her frame, leaving her ashen face and flaccid, with her lavender hair exposed. Reid's heart clenched as he raised her knuckles to his lips.

Lady Ismara had said they would do everything in their power to heal her and restore her energy, but the prospect of recovery grew slimmer. It seemed Selene's life hung by a thread most days, but Reid counted each of her breaths with a grateful prayer.

It had been a week since she had saved him and the children from Thalandros, and he hadn't left her side.

Petunia crawled off his arm and padded toward Selene. She sniffed and licked her cheek before curling
into a ball under Selene's jaw.

"I know, I miss her too," he said. "Looks like we both
grew fond of her."

One of Petunia's eyes peeked open into slits,
side-eyeing him. He chuckled.

"Fine... I grew more than fond of her. If you want me
to get sappy, I can, but I didn't think you'd like that."

Petunia's eyes closed as if satisfied, grinding her teeth
happily.

"You're bruxing, girl? Well, I can't say no to that. If you
must know..." Reid paused and took in Selene's slender
nose, her high cheekbones, and her pert mouth, usually
a rosy hue but now chapped and pale. Still, she remained
the most beautiful woman he'd ever beheld.

"I am hopelessly, stupidly, and fiercely in love with
her," he said, and leaned forward to settle his head next
to Selene. "Look at her, Petunia. I never stood a chance,
did I? I was supposed to be the villain of her story, but it
seems she was the better thief in the end. Stealing hearts
isn't an easy task, you know? But she can keep my heart
for however long she likes..."

"What about forever?"

Reid's head shot up, his mouth agape. Petunia stood,
alert, her eyes bulging in excitement. Selene's eyes fluttered open, her voice a mere rasp, but he'd give up every
coin, song, and dream he had to hear it again.

"A thief and an eavesdropper?" he tutted, but his heart
rang out in song with every beat. "You're more dangerous than I thought. First, you steal my heart, and

then you catch me at an embarrassingly sentimental moment?"

Selene smiled weakly.

"Nothing is embarrassing about what you said," she whispered.

"No? What's embarrassing is confessing such things to my rat friend rather than being man enough to say them to you while you're... y'know, conscious."

"I am now."

Her blue eyes sparkled up at him, and his breath caught in his throat.

Reid reached for her delicate hand and squeezed it gently. "Then... I hope you know how much I've been worried sick over you. You foolish... *wonderful* woman. For a moment, I thought I had lost you—"

Reid's voice hitched. He swallowed thickly, unable to stomach the rest of that thought. Selene rubbed the back of his hand, and he took a deep breath.

"You can't do that to me again. Never again. I need you now. You are my song—the music that keeps me sane—and I cannot live without you."

"Reid..."

"All that to say... I love you, Selene."

A small gasp escaped her parted lips. Her eyes brightened like sapphires under the glossy sheen of tears.

"So that kiss meant something to you?" she asked, her voice dipping hesitantly.

Reid chuckled breathlessly. Slowly, he leaned in and cradled her cheek in his palm. Their mouths met in a tender caress. Soft, deliberate, and filled with all the love he had—and all the love he longed to share with her.

When he parted, his forehead rested against hers. "It meant everything to me."

Her soft sigh tickled his cheek. "I love you, too."

"Do you know what that means?"

Selene's eyes flickered over his face, her brows scrunching. "What?"

"You're stuck with me, now."

Another smile bloomed on her lips. "I don't mind the sound of that."

A knock echoed at the door. Reid sat back in the chair as Lady Lysandriel strode into the room.

Her deep, warm eyes assessed them with a quiet, calm expression. "I see you're awake at last. I hope I wasn't interrupting anything?"

"Nothing we'd like you to see, at least," Reid teased.

Selene rolled her eyes but straightened in bed. "Lady Lysandriel. It is an honor to be in your presence. How may I be in your service?"

"You've already done a great service, Selene," Lysandriel said, leaning against her white, three-starred staff. "You have apprehended the true villain. We wish to bestow your wand back into your care."

Selene's eyes widened before they fell to her lap. Reid frowned. He had thought she would be more elated at the news.

"What's wrong?" he asked gently.

"I still haven't redeemed myself," Selene whispered.

"You have done what we have asked of you, child," Lysandriel said. "But redemption comes from the Divine and within you. What disturbs your peace?"

Selene took a deep, steadying breath. "I haven't atoned for what I've done. At least, not yet. I still wish to make amends."

Reid smiled, his chest warming with pride. This was the woman he fell in love with—the woman behind the chipped, perfectionist walls. It was about time his Violet bloomed into the extraordinary being she was always meant to be.

27

Selene regretted the crushing heartbreak that vibrated through her soul when an agonized howl echoed through the night.

The prince had found someone he truly loved. Selene watched the woman flee past the castle gates, her dark hair whipping in the wind, to return home.

Her heart clenched with shame, but most of all, guilt.

How could jealousy and rage have blinded her to lash out at an innocent being? The anger she had directed toward him was misplaced. All her insecurities, shame, and loneliness were due to a lifetime of proving herself to a man who would never be satisfied. The prince did not deserve this fate—he did not deserve to perish as a beast.

And Selene was determined to do everything in her power to ensure he never would.

Selene followed the woman named Rosabelle. She had striking, intelligent, rosy eyes, a magenta sheen to her dark locks, and a timeless beauty that Selene would have envied four months ago. The woman cried and laughed when she reunited with her family, and her father embraced her, peppering kisses into her hair. Selene watched from a distance until night fell.

She knew the prince did not have much time, but she couldn't intervene yet, not when Rosabelle deserved this brief moment with her family she'd been separated from. Selene had gathered enough intel to know what she needed to fix what she had broken.

When the moon was highest in the sky, Selene closed her eyes and breathed a spell under her breath. Lysandriel had removed her brand, which limited her structured magic, and ensured the best medical stewards gave her the strength to do this task.

Selene channeled her senses into the chilled wind rattling through the dark trees. Evarandor, a northern kingdom, was blanketed in snow even in early autumn. Her breath came out in quiet, white puffs against the falling snow, but warmth radiated through her core. A snowflake landed in her open palm, dissolving into liquid gold. It grew brighter, glowing like a tiny sun dancing against her fingers until it was swept into the frigid breeze. The light flittered into the sky, following an invisible path down the chimney and into a quiet, candlelit room.

The scent of parchment and melted beeswax filled the space, and a woman sat hunched over a book in a plush chair in the corner.

Rosabelle startled, shooting to her feet when she spied Selene's orb of magical light, sparkling like diamonds across an inky sky. The light encircled the woman and shot toward the door. Rosabelle followed with furrowed brows, down the stairs, across the hall, and opened the front door. Her footsteps crunched against the snow, and her eyes widened when she spotted Selene. The orb of light dimmed, disappearing into dust into Selene's palm.

She approached the woman who eyed her warily, her deep, plum cloak trailing behind her.

"W-who are you?" Rosabelle asked, clutching her shivering hands up at her chest.

"I'm a friend and a stewardess," Selene smiled ruefully, stopping a comfortable distance away. She did not wish to frighten the woman more than necessary.

"What do you want?"

"The beast—the prince is in peril. He has but a few hours before he meets his fate. Only you can save him, and you must go to him before dusk settles over the mountains tomorrow."

Rosabelle's eyes widened. "Did he know?"

Selene nodded somberly. "Yes. He let you go out of his love for you. If you love him in return, go to him before the last rose petal burns to ash."

Rosabelle stiffened, and an uneasy hush fell over the frigid space between them. Then, without warning or another word, Rosabelle dashed toward the stables, readying her horse and galloping into the night. She hadn't hesitated. Selene blinked, surprised but relieved that the woman understood the urgency of her task.

Selene raised a hand over her anxious heart and followed on her own steed. Along the journey, she uttered more spells, gifting the horse the stamina and speed Rosabelle needed to arrive in time.

The woman needed to prove her love and complete the journey alone.

Hours later, Selene stood within the shadows of the castle hall, hiding behind one of the marble pillars. Cheers echoed throughout the spacious room, and servants hugged one another, crying into each other's arms. In the center of the sparkling, stone floor, Prince Leander swung Rosabelle around in his arms, laughing with tears trickling down his face. Rosabelle squealed in delight, embracing him tightly.

A bottle of champagne exploded as servants toasted in celebration. Despite the joyous occasion, Selene hesitated. Her heart pounded painfully against her ribcage, but she forced herself from the shadows.

An eerie hush fell over the room as her heels clacked against the stone. Servants backed away, allowing her space, and she inwardly cringed. She deserved this—the gasps of fear, and the terrified sheen in their eyes. The moment Prince Leander lay eyes on her, he scowled, shielding Rosabelle with his body.

"Selene," he said her name like a hiss. "Why are you here?"

"I've come to make amends," Selene started gently, hoping to put him at ease.

"She's the woman," Rosabelle gasped, tugging on his sleeve. "She was the one who told me to come back to you before the last rose petal turned to ash."

Leander's eyes widened before narrowing as he turned to Selene. "I don't understand. After everything you've done, why would you do this?"

Selene bowed her head. "Because I am sorry for cursing you. I know I cannot erase my sins or how deeply they've affected you all, but I couldn't stand by and watch the happiness be ripped from you again. I do not ask for forgiveness. I came to apologize and hope you may live the life you've always dreamt of—the life I tried to destroy."

Silence weighed like a sullen cloud over the hall. Leander regarded her warily, his jaw ticking. Selene braced herself for the yelling, screaming, and curses flung her way—she would endure them all, for it was the least she deserved.

"What you did was a terrible thing," Leander said, finally breaking the tense silence.

Selene wouldn't run away from her shame. "Yes, it was."

Leander exhaled a long sigh, his shoulders slumped, and his gaze turned to Rosabelle. "But, you brought her back to me," he said. "And for that... I thank you. I don't know how long it will take me to forgive you, but I am grateful you brought us together."

Selene frowned. Was that all? Surely she deserved more vitriol from him. "You don't need to hold back. You may say whatever you wish to say to me, and I will hear it all."

"That's the thing," he smiled softly, and laced his fingers with Rosabelle. "Tonight, I have no room for hatred in my heart. I am simply overjoyed to have her back with me."

Selene's mouth quivered. "It was the least I could have done. If there is anything else I may do, please do not hesitate to ask."

Leander paused, seeming to mull the offer over. "I do have one request."

"Anything. Say the word."

"Please leave and never return."

Selene bowed, swallowing back the guilt-filled tears from spilling. "As you wish," she whispered.

Selene fell into Reid's arms when she returned, her sobs muffled into his velvet vest. Gently, he stroked her hair and shimmied them over to sit on the infirmary bed. Exhaustion tore through her limbs from her task, but the tears continued to swell.

"I know, that was very difficult," he said. "But I'm proud of you."

"It was but..." she sniffed, blinking the tears away. "I'm just so relieved I came in time. I don't know what I would have done if they hadn't broken the curse. I shudder at the thought. The guilt would have eaten me alive."

Reid's arms tightened around her. "But you made it."

"They are truly meant for each other," she said with a watery smile.

Selene inhaled his familiar, comforting sandalwood scent—the notes of forest and music clinging to his skin. It calmed the barrage of guilt and disgrace warring in her heart. She knew she had the rest of her life to continue atoning for her actions, but she thanked the Divine that she could begin by reuniting Prince Leander with his true love.

"I'm so glad you came into my life," she whispered against him.

"More like, you stormed into mine," Reid chuckled, and her cheek bounced against the reverberations in his chest. He pulled back to peer down at her with a soft grin. "You're the one who crashed my performance, remember?"

Selene bit back a smile. "Well, you didn't make it easy to find you."

"Of course not, where's the fun in that? I like the chase." He winked.

Heat flushed through her cheeks, her eyes darting to his lips. "Is the chase still on?"

Warmth simmered in his gaze as he drew in closer. "No, I've been thoroughly and happily captured by the woman I love. I have no regrets."

"Neither do I," she whispered.

His mouth met hers, and she sighed happily against him. It was slow, gentle, and reverent. The kind of kiss where he seemed to savor and memorize every curve of her lips and the rhythm of her breaths. Selene wrapped her arms around his neck, letting the world vanish as she clung to him. In this moment, and the many moments to come, she knew she had found where she belonged.

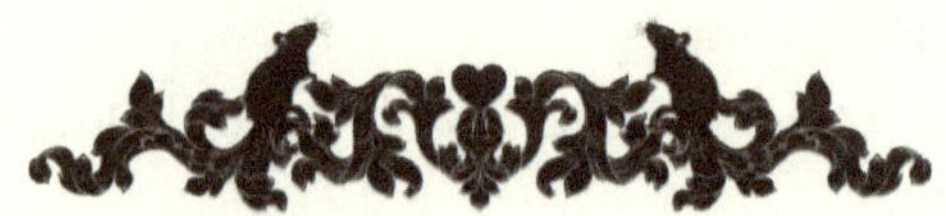

One Year Later

"Settle down, children," Selene said. She waved her purple wand, and the weight of it, adorned with a crescent moon and scattered stars, settled against her skin like a gentle embrace.

The children scrambled and wiggled in their seats, ready for the lesson she prepared.

"Today's lesson is on wild magic. Can anyone tell me its purpose?"

A child with curly blond hair eagerly raised her hand.

"Yes, Georgette?"

"Wild magic is the magic intwined with Lioren. It is unrestrained and dangerous if used improperly."

"Correct. And how does that differ from structured magic?" Selene asked.

Georgette raised her hand again, but she called on the red-haired boy who reminded her of a certain Pied Piper.

"Yes, Florien?"

"Structured magic comes from within, but mostly from the Divine. It is trained through wands."

"Very good, now let's open our books to chapter thirty-two. We'll be exploring more about wild magic this afternoon..."

The lesson continued, and before she knew it, the hour had passed too soon.

"Now, don't forget, your homework—" she started.

"Is to turn your teacher's apple into a frog."

Selene placed her hands on her hips, playfully scowling at the man leaning casually against the doorframe. His easy smile and warm glint in his eye melted some of her annoyance.

"Is to study up on chapter thirty-three," Selene corrected. Some of the boys groaned, whispering how they'd rather practice magic on apples. "Mr. Pfeiffer is jesting. Now, run along. And don't forget to practice channeling your structured magic!"

"Yes, Mrs. Pfeiffer!" they cried.

The herd of children ran past Reid, and he sauntered in with a smirk.

His strong hands found her waist, but she gave him a playful nudge. "I thought you were supposed to be teaching your Enchanted Music class."

"I was, but I came to say hello to my beautiful wife."

Selene raised a brow. "You can't keep ending them early just to say hello to me."

He shrugged, and Petunia popped from his collar, her whiskers quivering.

"Are you putting him up to this?" she asked the rat.

"No, she's a goody-two-shoes, like you."

Petunia crawled on his shoulder, squeaking protests with her paws on her hips. After spending time with the rat, Selene learned to decipher her chittering language.

"And what's wrong with that, Reid? What do you have against following rules?" Petunia huffed and glanced at Selene. *"The things we put up with."*

Reid chuckled, shaking his head. "I suppose you two do put up with a lot, I'll give you that."

Selene giggled, "Well, it seems you could learn a thing or two from us."

"And stop being the fun teacher? I'll pass," he said with a smirk.

Selene rolled her eyes, huffing under her breath. However, she couldn't stay annoyed when one hand cupped her belly. The little one within her responded with a kick to their father's touch. Reid's smile bloomed as he reached for her face.

"You're staring at me," she murmured.

He leaned in, his dark cherry hair sweeping against her forehead. "Can you blame me?"

"Reid—"

"I've been waiting to do this all morning," he whispered against her lips. He swiftly silenced her objections with a sound, gentle kiss. Selene couldn't help but lean in, her eyes fluttering closed as he wrapped his arms around her.

"Ewww!"

Selene jerked away from Reid's grasp. A crowd of children peeked from the door, giggling and making mock gagging noises. She smiled, despite her embarrassed flush creeping on her cheeks. The children from Hamlin had integrated well with the other children learning at the Arcane Sanctum. They found a home where they would never be taken advantage of again.

"They're kissing!" a little girl named Kalia laughed.

"Do you want to see it again?" Reid asked, leaning in.

Selene placed her hand over his mouth, pushing him away, but the little girls cooed.

"Do you think their baby will have magenta hair?" one girl whispered.

"I think so!" another chirped.

"Off you go," Selene said, shooing them. The children scampered away, whispering and giggling as they made their way down the hall. Once they were out of sight, she sighed, but a grin tugged on her lips.

"Now, where were we, Selene?" Reid asked, his hands anchoring over her waist.

Selene shook her head, expelling a breathy laugh. "You're shameless, aren't you?"

"Only for you. And funny enough, you're still here," he whispered in her ear. His fingers played with the hairs on the back of her neck in soothing motions. She leaned into him, relishing his warmth and the fortress of his arms around her.

"I am. And I always will be."

Thank you for reading *Falling for the Pied Piper*!

To learn more about my books and stay connected, join my newsletter and claim a FREE Cinderella short story. A Charming Dance is a prequel to A Charming Hope that you don't want to miss out on. Visit my website, check out my author pages on Amazon and Goodreads, and follow me on all my social media platforms like Instagram and Facebook @ashleyevercott.author .

I hope you will kindly consider leaving a review. Reviews not only help authors find new readers, but they also help readers find new books to enjoy. Thank you so much!

Want more no-spice fairy tale mash-ups where the villains finally get their chance at a happily ever after? Check out the rest of the To Win a Dark Heart multi-author collection!

Falling for the Trickster by Lucy Tempest (Rumpelstiltskin + Goose Girl)

Falling for the Doomed Bride by C.K. Beggan (Bluebeard + Sleeping Beauty)

Falling for the Winged Witch by Sarah Beran (Wild Swans + Jack & the Beanstalk)

Falling for the Crystal Fae by Anabelle Raven (The Snow Queen + Aladdin)

Falling for the Pirate by Nicki Chapelway (Peter Pan + The Little Mermaid)

Falling for the Mad King by Sydney Winward (Alice in Wonderland + The 12 Dancing Princesses)

Falling for the Sorcerer by Jes Drew (Rapunzel + Swan Lake)

Falling for the Wolf by Megan Charlie (Little Red Riding Hood + Cinderella)

Falling for the Enchantress by Lyndsey Hall (Robin Hood + King Arthur)

Falling for the Pied Piper by Ashley Evercott (Beauty & the Beast + The Pied Piper)

Falling for the Dark Mage by Lucy Winton (East of the Sun, West of the Moon + The Frog Prince)

Falling for the Huntsman by Leialoha Humpherys (Snow White + Hansel & Gretel)

This book wouldn't be possible without so many people to cheer me on. Thank you to my husband, the Once Upon a Pen Community, Scarlett and Elaine. Thank you Sydney, for critiquing my work and helping my book shine. Thank you, Emerald Editing, for your services and being a wonderful editor. Thank you to MoorBooks Design for the amazing cover. Last but not least, thank you, readers, for reading *Falling for the Pied Piper*. I couldn't do it without any of you.

Fairy Tales of Gallia
Enchanting Fate: A Beauty and the Beast Retelling
Enchanting Thorns: A Sleeping Beauty Retelling

Hope Ever After (also included in the Fairy Tales of Gallia Series)
A Charming Hope: A Frog Prince Retelling

The Haunted Brew
Horsemen and Hot Chocolate: A Legend of Sleepy Hollow Retelling

Ashley Evercott was born and raised where it's mostly sunny and there's always traffic on the 91. From a young age, she has dreamed of far-off worlds and star-crossed lovers. She is proud to pen these stories to life. When she is not writing, she is consuming as many books as she can and daydreaming at home with her cat and supportive husband.

ashleyevercott.com
ashleyevercott@gmail.com